RIDERS IN THE NIGHT

The man in the living armor nodded. "You should get some rest. Tomorrow—" He looked up sharply, turned towards the window.

Mezka stifled a yelp.

The man in the living armor crossed the room in a single stride. Pressing himself against the far wall he peered out the window. Mezka heard him suck in his breath. Extracting herself from the sand, she moved to stand beside him.

Tiny lights bobbed within the forest of cacti. As Mezka watched they began to emerge, first one, then another, and then another. Soon there were nine of them moving in single file. As they drew closer Mezka saw that each of the lights belonged to a man who sat perched upon a long-necked hýthric. Some of the men rode tall in the saddle, others were small and bent. One of them had two arms on his left side; another had a single horn growing from the middle of his forehead.

"Deviants."

The man in the living armor did not spit out the word like so many others would have. Instead he simply stated a fact. A moment later he stated another.

"This will not end well."

DAUGHTER OF AGONIES

G. Owen Wears

For everyone who has found something
of value in my work.

CONTENTS

INTRODUCTION

"The Pellucid Witch" was a greater success than I had anticipated. That's not to say I broke any sales records, however the book did garner a small following. Not bad for a pulp adventure story I bashed out just for the hell of it. Naturally, this prompted me to write a sequel.

The idea for another of Krýl's adventures had been knocking around in my head since I debuted the first few installments of "The Pellucid Witch" in my anthology, "Exterus". At the time I wasn't sure where this concept might lead, but I had some very clear ideas about a girl, a belt of skulls, a forest of cacti, and an outpost. When I sat down to write, I just let these concepts go where they would. The result was a good one. Or at least so I thought.

High on my own perceived prowess as a writer, I sent the book off for copy-editing and went to the movies. The particular film I saw made me cradle my head in my hands and say several very nasty words.

Some of the key concepts around which I'd built the character of Krýl were splashed across the silver screen with reckless abandon. There were sharpened tentacles galore and a semi-parasitic relationship between the main character and his symbiote. While not an exact match, there was enough crossover that anyone with eyes will be able to make a connection between my book and this film.

The thought of being seen as a rip-off artist was something that worried me mightily. I fussed and fumed over this potential blow to my credibility for days. At last I settled down and took a deep breath. No one had said anything nasty online and none of my readers had called me out. And, if I'm being honest, the comic this film was based on actually influenced my own creation. It had been twenty-odd years since I'd come up with Krýl, but the connection was there.

From the 1930s to the 1990s, from Japan to the USA, there are a multitude of works that influenced this book and its predecessor. I drew on these stories not because I couldn't be bothered to come up with my own ideas, but because the source material had sparked something in my imagination. That something grew and changed, was added to, and changed again. By the end of the process, I was looking at a world and a set of characters that were uniquely my own.

Using this world I built on the shoulders of giants as a backdrop, I've done my best to tell a compelling story. If I've done my job correctly it is the characters that readers will remember, not just the strange creatures or the blood-splattered environs. While sequences involving Krýl's fungoid armor are incredibly fun to write, it's the man inside that armor that I've tried to focus on. His traveling companion Mezka even more so. She's an ordinary girl caught in extraordinary circumstances. One of the greatest challenges of writing this book was trying to walk in her footsteps while she led Krýl from one burning desert to the next. I certainly hope I've done these characters justice and that I've created a story that will spark something in the imaginations of my own readers.

G. Owen Wears
December 2021

THE SETTLEMENT

One

She walked six paces ahead, sandaled feet on bare earth, deftly picking her way between the cacti. At twice her height, the forest of cladodes crowded one against the other, sectioning the carmine light into patches. Around every turn spines as long as her arm reached for the girl. When they drew too near she would press the spines out of her way, leaving them to quiver and shake. The contents of the gourd tied to the stick slung over her shoulder sloshed despite her careful steps. The symbiote told Krýl to take the gourd. Krýl told the symbiote to be silent.

Dust clung to the hem of the girl's robe, denuded yellow against faded black. Her hood was up, dark hair hidden beneath loose folds of threadbare wool. Only her slender ankles were visible, light brown skin wrapped in dark brown leather. The symbiote urged Krýl to take the girl as well.

Again he told the symbiote to be silent.

Something touched his shoulder. A cactus spine as thick as Krýl's thumb grated across the scarred carapace that covered him from head to toe. Krýl reached up and snapped it off. The cactus quaked and the empty areole oozed green. Stretching out his hand, Krýl prompted the eukaryotic shell to extend a hollow spine of its own, a feeding tube. It obliged, plunging the spike into the wound he had made. Krýl felt the symbiote relax, and the moisture it took in kept it occupied just long enough for him to silence its grumbling.

Slithering out of the north and east, a hot breath of wind set the cacti in motion. It hummed through their spines and made their shadows gambol and sway. Her pace still unvaried, the girl stepped deftly around bristling clumps and clusters, her robe miraculously free of snags. Krýl withdrew the feeding spike just as the girl disappeared behind a cluster of cacti. He caught her up a moment later.

"How much further?"

The girl did not turn to look at him, simply kept moving, one foot following the other.

"It's well past midday."

The girl lifted her free hand. She held up three fingers.

"What does that mean?"

The girl wiggled the fingers.

"Three? Three what?"

"It means we will be there soon." The girl let her hand drop.

"How soon is soon?"

For a long while the girl did not speak. She rolled her narrow hips, the water gourd swinging from the stick over her shoulder. At last she said, "Soon."

Krýl reached for the girl's shoulder, then stopped and withdrew his hand. The girl had said six paces. She had said that was proper. She had said she would guide him; in return he would pay her and he would keep the six paces.

A shadow passed overhead. Krýl looked up and the membranes over his eyes darkened. Peering skyward he watched as a pair of silhouettes wafted their way from south to north. Their flight was languid, a three count between each beat of their wings. Catching the thermals rising from the distant hardpan they began to climb. In lazy circles they rose towards the bloated red ball of the sun.

"Vermin."

The symbiote echoed Krýl's sentiment.

It took another thousand steps before the first of the cactus flowers showed orange and violet against the profusion of yellow spines. It was as large as Krýl's fist, hanging just above head height. Without breaking stride the girl lifted one thin hand and brushed the petals. The flower bobbed, a dusting of pollen falling from its stamen.

The girl moved on, slipped around another stand of cacti. Krýl followed, glancing at the flower as he passed. The armor suggested eating it. As more blooms appeared, Krýl considered giving in and letting it gorge itself. The thought was short lived. Better not to allow the symbiote free rein. The more it ate, the harder it would be to rein it back in.

Another hundred paces and the cacti began to thin. More light reached the parched ground, the red blotches beginning to outnumber the darker patches of shade. Here the cacti were smaller, their color a jaundiced yellow rather than pale green. When they were short enough to see over, the girl stopped. Krýl stepped up beside her.

"There." The girl pointed.

Krýl snorted. "I didn't need you to tell me that. I've got eyes."

The girl slid the stick from her shoulder, tucked the flat

of one foot against her knee, and leaned on the smooth length of wood.

Krýl crossed his arms. "It's the only settlement we've seen for two days."

The girl did not reply. In the hot, still air her dusty robe hung wrinkled and listless about her slight frame.

The settlement sat on an incline tucked against a striated wall of rock. The sandstone cliff was the color of the cactus flowers, orange with streaks of violet. Waves of heat rose from the rock face, making it appear to quaver and shift.

Shading her eyes, the girl looked towards the west. "Sundown, two hours."

Krýl checked the angle of the shadows. "Maybe less."

Ahead the collection of low buildings were piled one atop the other, a haphazard jumble of sandstone and decaying granite. Encircling the settlement was a wall made of the same. The gate that broke the shallow curve of the wall was narrow and pointed at the top. It stood open and unguarded.

"If I didn't know better I'd say they were expecting us."

"They are not."

"You sure?"

The girl tapped the side of her head with one slender finger. Krýl grunted.

"Besides," the girl nodded towards the gate, "the hinges are empty. The doors are gone."

Krýl squinted at the sandstone arch. The girl was right; the brass hinges hung loose from their fittings, broken and tarnished.

The girl took a step forward. Krýl put a hand on her shoulder.

"I'll go first."

"Why?"

Krýl turned his armored face towards the diminutive figure in black. "Because I said I'll go first."

The girl lifted her hand and made a small gesture.

As the last of the cacti grew small and fell behind, the wind began to rise. Grains of sand hissed and clattered against the hard surface of the armor. Krýl tugged at the tattered remains of his cloak. Buckling it shut, he pulled up the hood, then checked to see if the girl was still there. She followed six paces behind, one hand holding her own hood in place.

Krýl angled his steps towards the gate, feet crunching over loose stones and the shells of beetles uncovered by the shifting sand. The wind drove the sand against the base of the wall, adding to the drifts that had already risen to half its height. Even if the gate had been intact, those drifts would have made the wall indefensible. Once it had served an important and obvious purpose. Now it was just in the way.

When he was directly under the sandstone arch Krýl stopped and looked up. He looked to the sides. There was no sign of scarring, no hunks of stone chiselled from the frame.

"Why would they take down their own gate?"

The girl stopped a few feet from Krýl and examined the empty hinges. "Wood has great value."

"As fuel?"

"As anything."

Shaking his head, Krýl stepped through.

A stretch of waste ground stood between the wall and the settlement. The remains of dugouts and makeshift shelters littered the spaces between rough outcroppings of stone. The occupants of this shanty town were nowhere in evidence. The only movement came from skittering rills of sand and the flap and flutter of tattered canvas.

Behind him Krýl heard the girl scuff to a halt and poke at something with her stick. When he turned around he saw her peering into one of the shelters.

"What do you see?"

The girl glanced up at him. "Bones."

"Human?"

The girl bobbed her fist.

Krýl turned around and started walking. The girl matched his pace, six steps behind.

A moment later and they were in the shade of the cliff. Here the temperature was almost bearable. Vents opened along Krýl's sides forcing out heat, drawing in the cooler air. He adjusted his cloak and checked its buckles.

The wind gusted and again Krýl glanced over his shoulder. In the east, above the forest of cacti, he could see rising clouds of dust.

"What is it?" asked the girl.

"Nothing."

The girl glanced at the dark smudge, then back at Krýl. "What are you looking for?"

"Crystals."

The girl sniffed. "No crystals. Not here."

Krýl spared the cloud of dust another glance, then rapped his knuckles on the carapace that covered his temple. The armor resisted for a moment, then peeled itself back from his head. As it went the symbiote gnawed at Krýl, siphoning off the nutrients needed to facilitate the change. In the pit of his stomach Krýl felt the familiar pang of being used as a larder for the ever-covetous armor. When the pain had fled, he continued on.

It took a moment for Krýl to realize he had managed to find his way onto a narrow street. Most of its length had been covered by sand, the desert slowly laying claim to the cobbles. The lane passed between two low buildings, their empty windows showing bare interiors—bare save for the drifts of sand piled in the corners.

Krýl indicated the one on the right. "If we can't find a bed in town we can always camp here. Good to have options, yeah?"

The girl said nothing.

As they walked the buildings grew taller, closer together. With each block the maze of alleyways and side streets became more and more convoluted. Rubbish began to appear, a few broken pieces of pottery, animal bones, the remains of a chamber pot and its contents. Krýl did his best not to step in any of it.

Moving with them down the narrow streets, the wind moaned and chuckled. It swirled in corners and brushed the faces of the buildings. Krýl watched the moving sand from behind a hand held before his face. The girl did the same, stepping where he stepped, using him as a windbreak. Krýl wished he could have left the armor in place. It would have done wonders to prevent sand from collecting on his lips and trying to crawl up his nose. Keep it in place, however, and he looked too much the outsider, too much the predator.

The first sign of life came in the form of a shadow. It touched a wall to Krýl's left then disappeared with the sound of a door being pulled shut. Another turn of the street and he caught sight of a figure draped in black, only the eyes showing above its veil.

Krýl motioned for the girl. Blinking sand from her eyelashes she stepped forward. Raising her hand she said something to the figure. The figure ignored her and continued on its way. The girl looked back at Krýl and moved her fist back and forth.

"Could she understand you?"

"I spoke in her language. She did not wish to speak it back."

Further up the street another figure emerged from a doorway, took note of them, and scuttled down an alley. The movement reminded Krýl of an insect.

"Where are they all going?"

The girl lifted her hand, palm out. "It is curfew. They must be indoors before the stars come out."

Another figure moved towards them through the failing light, an amphora balanced on one hip. Krýl gestured towards her with his chin. "Ask her where the well is."

The girl did so. The figured raised her hand, said something in response. The woman's voice was deep, but her tone clipped. She then slipped past Krýl and the girl.

"The well is not for outsiders," said the girl. "If we want water we will have to buy it."

"Where?"

The girl indicated another side street.

"Is that where he would have gone, to buy water?"

"The man you are following?"

Krýl nodded. "That's the one."

A vicious gust sent the girl's robe streaming out beside her. Krýl moved around the girl and set himself between her and the wind. When the gust finally died she turned her dark eyes up to his, raised her fist, and dipped it twice.

"Then that's where we'll go."

Two

"You can pay in barter, you can pay in metal, or you can pay in flesh. The choice is yours."

Krýl regarded the man. The man stared right back at him. His thin face was expressionless, his black hair slick and shiny against his skull. His beard was neat and close-cropped.

"I have coin."

"That's good." The man's eyes remained fixed on Krýl.

"How much?"

"An ingot."

Krýl broke eye contact and shook his head. "Too much."

The man stood, put his hands against the small of his back, and stretched. "This is not a bazaar; we do not haggle here. The price is what the price is."

Krýl looked over at the girl. She stood against the far wall of the small stone room staring down at the floor. He jabbed a thumb in her direction. "She needs water."

"So do we all." The man reached to one side and picked up a gourd. He drank from it, went to set it aside, then raised it and drank from it again.

Krýl swallowed in sympathy and felt the dryness in his own throat.

"The price is too much."

The water seller chuckled. "It is. But if you want water you will pay it."

Krýl scratched at the back of his neck. The eukaryotic shell was trying to work its way back up the collar of his cloak. He told it to remain where it was.

The man smiled, spread his hands. "You must drink, I must drink, she must drink. The price is worth it."

Reaching under his cloak, Krýl came out with a full ingot. He gave it to the man. The man examined it, bit it, and smiled. Reaching around behind him he rapped his knuckles against a heavy door banded with brass. A hole with a shutter opened in the door. The man said something, the hole closed, and a slot at waist height opened. A litre of water was passed through and the man took it. He handed it to Krýl.

"You may keep the container. We make them out of hollow gourds."

"How kind."

The man placed his hand over his heart and inclined his head. "I live to serve."

Sucking one canine tooth, Krýl turned towards the girl. He handed her the gourd then started for the door. After three steps he stopped and turned back towards the water seller.

"How many customers have you had today? How many yesterday?"

The man lifted an eyebrow. "Eventually everyone comes through my door."

"How many have been through your door recently?"

"Recently? Couldn't say." The water seller smiled again, his dark eyes still without expression.

Krýl dug inside his cloak and brought out another ingot.

The water seller laughed and held up his hand. "I really couldn't say."

Krýl moved to the door and together he and the girl stepped from the little room and back onto the street.

"You could have said something."

With the gourd held in the crook of one arm, the girl glanced up at Krýl. "He would not have spoken to me."

"Why not?"

"I am female. I have no cast."

Krýl glanced at her out of the corner of his eye. "The men here won't talk to you?"

"Some of them will. Not him. He is Kommhadi. The women we saw earlier are Kommhadi as well."

"Are all the people here Kommhadi?"

This time when she spoke the girl did not look up. "Not all of them."

The wind gusted, not as fiercely as before but strong enough to make both Krýl and the girl close their eyes and turn their heads. Krýl contemplated raising the carapace to cover his face. He decided against it and made do with his hood.

With darkness fast approaching, the streets had become even more labyrinthine, shadows crowding out the corners and curves. Krýl doubted if he could find his way out of the settlement on his own. Not without blundering about for most of the night. Here and there patches of light crept from under doors or through cracks in shutters pulled tight against the wind. Where the streets had not been plunged into total darkness, the walls of the surrounding buildings had become a uniform gray. Trailing his fingers along their pitted surface, Krýl felt the residual heat of the day lingering in the stones.

"The man I'm after, he'll need a place to sleep."

The girl shifted the weight of the new water gourd, balancing it against her stick. "He will."

"Where?"

The girl gestured with her right hand.

"You must have some idea. You've been here before, not me."

The girl thought for a moment. "That does not mean I know where he will sleep."

Krýl opened his mouth for a rebuttal, but the sound of the girl's stomach cut him short. The sound of it grumbling cut even through the hiss and moan of the wind.

"When was the last time you ate?"

The girl moved her hand from side to side and indicated the gourd Krýl had bought. "It does not matter. I have water."

"Water won't do you much good on its own."

Again the girl moved her hand. "You are the one with money."

Krýl glanced up at the thin sliver of sky visible between the walls of cut stone. There were no stars, not yet.

"Where do they sell food at this time of day?"

"The bilaza."

"Show me."

"I am not hungry." The girl's stomach growled again, making a liar out of her.

"Well, I am hungry." Krýl stared down the narrow street. "So show me."

Lowering her head, the girl stepped and ducked into the shadows. Krýl followed. He lost track of the twists and turns within a few dozen paces. At last they emerged into a cramped little square. Like the cobbled road leading to the settlement it had been paved, and like the road, the desert had done its best to swallow it. Sand had found its way between the stones and sat in drifts against the windward sides of the buildings. At one end was a tea house, its door open, the light of an oil lamp spilling onto the pavement. At the other end was a cart illuminated by a pair of tapers. From it came the smell of cooking. In the center of the square stood an iron scaffold bolted to a stone pillar.

Ignoring the pillar, Krýl pointed to the tea house, then the cart. Without bothering to respond, the girl made her way to the cart.

She was already in conversation with the vendor when Krýl stepped up behind her. The man was short, balding, a thick moustache hiding his upper lip. The girl gestured towards Krýl with her head. The man looked up at him.

"Pay him."

"For what?"

"For the food you want."

"And what sort of food do I want?"

"Fried cactus blossoms."

Krýl looked down at the girl, sniffed at the frying cactus blossoms. "Order another serving and ask him about our friend."

The girl did and Krýl paid the man. In return he gave them clay bowls filled with fried cactus blossoms and a dull shake of the head. Krýl had the first blossom halfway to his mouth when the wind tried to take it from him. He turned away and covered the bowl with his body. The girl did the same. The man behind the cart lost his tapers, the wind snuffing the tiny flames. He grumbled something and took them down. Touching the ends of the tapers to the fire bowl hidden in his cart he set them back in their holders.

Before the wind could make another attempt at his dinner, Krýl shoved a cactus blossom into his mouth. It burned his tongue and forced him to chew with his mouth open. Shaking her hand, the girl moved past him, making her way towards the center of the bilaza. Tucking another cactus blossom into his mouth, Krýl sauntered after. The symbiote wriggled, but kept its place, for once not begrudging him a meal of his own.

The girl stopped in front of the iron scaffolding set halfway between the cart and the tea house. Chewing thoughtfully, she looked up at the creaking, groaning thing. Krýl followed her gaze.

The scaffolding had been designed to look like a tree of sorts. Instead of leaves or fruit hanging from its branches, it sprouted cages—five of them. The column of stone served as the trunk of the tree, the scaffolding riveted and pinned to the living rock. The cages were all set at different heights, perhaps to economize for space, perhaps just for the sake of aesthetics. Currently two of the cages were occupied.

Krýl stepped closer and felt the symbiote stir. Opening the vents along his sides it sampled the air. A moment later and the vents had closed, the armor again dormant. Squinting into the gloom Krýl saw why.

The occupants of the cages were little more than dry skin stretched over dry bone. The bones themselves looked as though they had been twisted out of true, sculpted into something less than human.

"Deviants," said the girl.

Krýl fished another blossom from his clay bowl. "Was that what earned them a place in these cages?"

"Yes." The girl emptied her own bowl. Krýl was not surprised to see it disappear as quickly as the others.

"I don't suppose they received much of trial."

The girl swallowed and wiped her mouth with the back of her wrist. "Best that you keep the thing you are wearing out of sight. If the Kommhadi see it they will put you in one of these cages."

Krýl chuckled. "They could try. Now what's say we go find out if our friend decided to stop for a cup of tea?"

In the tight space between two narrow walls and down a flight of worn steps, the wind was not as bad. The rubbish in the alley was old and dry, smelling of nothing more than dust and the desert. There were beetle shells here as well. They crackled underfoot, were ground to dust, and carried off by the wind.

"Perhaps he's not much of a tea drinker."

The girl looked at him sideways.

Krýl raised an eyebrow. "What?"

"Everyone drinks tea."

"Not everyone."

"Here, in this place, everyone drinks tea."

"What about cactus juice?"

"What do you think the tea was sweetened with?"

Krýl's toe caught a loose cobble and he stumbled. Putting out his hand he caught himself against the wall of the building to his right.

The girl stopped and stood, her stick held in one hand, the gourd of water they had purchased in the other.

"Don't look at me like that."

The girl continued to stand and stare.

"Just because I have this thing on me doesn't mean I can see in the dark or that I'm immune from stubbing my toe."

The girl remained mute.

Krýl straightened. "We asked the water seller. He said nothing. We asked the man who sold us the cactus blossoms. He said nothing. We asked at the tea house. Still nothing. I'm beginning to think we're going about this the wrong way."

The girl tugged at the neck of her robe and adjusted her hood. "What makes you say that?"

"No one is speaking to us."

"Perhaps we are not asking the right questions."

"This is your part of the world so you tell me, what sort of questions should we be asking?"

"None."

"What do you mean none?" Krýl bit back the urge to shout. Only just. In a forced whisper he said, "That doesn't make any sense."

The girl looked down the darkened street, then up at the sky. The moon had crawled its way past the horizon and most of the way into the sky. Its light was tainted by the dust in the air, its color a sickly orange.

"Your speech is too plain."

Krýl felt his upper lip pull back from his teeth. "How else should I speak?"

"With tact."

"Tact will get us nowhere."

"We are nowhere now."

Along his back the symbiote wriggled. Krýl felt a wave crawl up the armor and towards his naked scalp.

"You are too quick to anger." The girl adjusted her grip on the water gourd. "I can see it in the way you stand, hear it in the way you talk. Others see it and hear it as well."

"We've been walking for nearly five days. My patience is wearing thin."

"This is the desert." The girl looked back over her shoulder. "Nothing comes quickly here except death."

Krýl laughed. He couldn't help himself. "I've crossed more deserts than the years you've been alive. But this man I'm looking for, he's not made of sand and sun. He's made of flesh and blood. If he came this way someone will have seen him. He's difficult to miss."

"As are you." Wearily the girl shrank against the wall Krýl had used to keep from falling. Her black robe merged with the shadows, turning her into another scrap of midnight.

"What is it?" Krýl glanced around, saw nothing.

The girl did not move.

The armor sent a warning up the back of his neck and Krýl pressed himself against the wall beside girl.

There were footsteps, six pairs of feet scuffing their way along the sandy street. Slowly Krýl turned his head towards the sound. A moment later a figure appeared at the end of the alley. It was followed by another. They spoke, then the two men turned towards a third man, this one carrying a torch. In its glow Krýl could see the face of the water seller.

Beside him, the girl sucked in a breath and held it. Krýl felt the armor send tendrils up the back of his skull and along his jaw, siphoning off bits of him as it went.

More words passed between the three men at the mouth of the alley. Krýl saw the water seller's eyes narrow and the corners of his mouth turn down. He pointed back the way he had come, then up the street. The sound of footsteps came again. A moment later and the water seller and his torch were out of sight.

The girl let out her breath, seeming to deflate. Krýl tried to convince the armor to stop its climb up his skull and failed. It continued to collect protein, calcium, and collagen until his face was fully covered. He sighed as shimmering membranes slipped over his eyes. When he looked down at the girl he could see her outlined clearly against the stone wall. The symbiote may have taken the few calories afforded him by the cactus blossoms, but at least he would not have to stumble around blind.

"We need to get off the street." The girl's voice was a croaky little whisper.

Krýl opened and closed his fist. He flexed his fingers. The symbiote urged him to follow the men, to drive a hollow spine into their chests and carve off bits of flesh.

"You're right," said Krýl, dropping his hand to his side. "We should go."

Three

The house stood at the edge of the settlement overlooking the shanty town. It had no door and its narrow window had no shutters. Sand had crept inside, piling itself along the walls and filling in the fire pit. That did not matter much; they had no wood to burn. Tainted streaks of moonlight stole through the open window throwing a horizontal bar across the floor.

The man in the living armor had positioned himself

beside the open window that looked out across the jumble of dugouts and collapsed tents. His silhouette appeared broken at the edges, as if brushing up against him would leave a body cut and bleeding. Mezka sat tucked against one of the miniature dunes and watched the man as he watched the desert.

Save for the wind tugging at an errant scrap of tarpaulin, nothing moved. Mezka listened to the canvas flutter and the sand skitter. The night had stolen the heat of the day, the faded orange moonlight a dim reminder of the pulsing red sun. Mezka shivered, wrapped her arms around her middle, and pulled her robe tighter.

The man in the living armor shifted his weight, his head tracking slowly from left to right. Mezka wondered if he was cold. He did not seem to mind the heat of the day and he was not shivering now.

"For a while I lived in a place where the sky was bright and clear."

Mezka looked up at the man. She sniffed, rubbed at her nose with a corner of her robe.

"Here there's too much dust in the air, but in that valley the moon cut the night into slivers of gray and black."

Mezka looked down at the floor. The orange rectangle of light had crept a little further. Not much, but a little.

"V-valley?" said Mezka through chattering teeth. "W-where?"

The man in the living armor waved a hand dismissively. "It was a long ways from here."

Mezka watched the rectangle of moonlight. In a little less than half an hour it would touch the hem of her robe.

"We need to go about this another way."

"G-go about what?"

The man in the living armor turned towards Mezka, stepping momentarily into the rectangle of light. The armor plating that covered his face was jagged and scarred, sectioned into overlapping planes. The membranes that covered his eyes were yellow and glassy.

"I asked questions, but no one answered. Not even when offered money."

Mezka shivered again and wrapped her arms that much tighter around her middle. She huddled further into the miniature dune. It was a poor substitute for a fire and a bed.

"Maybe tomorrow I should ask harder."

"M-maybe tomorrow you should n-not ask at all."

The man tilted his head to the side, the moonlight reflecting from one yellow eye.

"Tact," said Mezka.

"What's that supposed to mean?"

"There is little p-point in asking the s-same questions again."

"Why?"

"Your words are in the air. You have already asked your questions and p-people have listened. T-they did not answer because you are not Kommhadi. They did not answer because you are an outsider. But they know that you are looking."

"And what about you? They know you're with me."

Mezka lifted her hand. "Y-yes, they know."

"So what now?"

Mezka went back to shivering.

The man in the living armor stepped away from the window. He crossed the space between them and knelt in front of her. Mezka heard the armor move as he moved, shift as he shifted. It opened a series of slits along the man's sides and she heard the intake of air.

"So, if everyone knows that we're here, and everyone knows that we're looking for someone, why bother with tact?

At this point it would be better to kick down a few doors and see if we can flush him out. Think of it like lifting a stone and watching the bugs wriggle out from beneath."

Mezka made a back-and-forth motion with her hand, frowned. "You can do this thing, but…"

"But what?"

"It would be best if we left soon after."

The man in the living armor snorted.

Mezka tugged at her hood, tried not to make eye contact with the man. "What m-makes you think he is s-still here?"

"Where else is he going to go?"

"Dhulkant is five days' ride from here."

"Less if we cross the hardpan."

Mezka kept her eyes on the floor.

"You've done it before, yes?"

"Yes. I did not have a choice." Mezka thought for a moment, then said, "He is important to you, this man you are following?"

The man in the living armor shook his head. Mezka thought it a gesture of negation, but she was not sure. He did a fair amount of head shaking.

"He wasn't important to me. Not at first"

"Then why follow him?"

"He was important to another."

"Is this other the one that gave you the ingots?"

"Yes."

"How many ingots?"

"Many."

"And there will be more?"

"If I bring this man in, yes."

"You do this for the ingots?"

The man in the living armor raised and lowered his head once. Mezka was reasonably certain this gesture was in the affirmative. "What do you call this thing that you do, following one man so you can deliver him to another?"

"Bounty."

Mezka rolled the word around in her head for a while, then looked back down at the bar of moonlight. It was closer now. Not much longer and it would begin to creep up her side.

The man in the living armor got to his feet. He tugged at the knots that held his ragged cloak around his shoulders. When it was free he held it out to her. Mezka looked at the tattered folds of cloth. She did not want to take it.

"I can hear your teeth chattering."

Mezka clamped her jaw shut.

The man in the living armor dropped the cloak in front of her. Mezka hesitated for a moment, then took it. She slung it over her shoulders and pulled it tight. The fabric smelled strange, like trail dust and something very, very old.

"This person you work for, why does he want this man you are following?"

The man in the living armor lifted his shoulders then let them fall. Mezka had seen this sort of thing before. It meant indecision or that he did not have an answer. Often when he did this the man in the living armor would give her an answer anyway.

"I didn't ask and my employer didn't say."

"Then why take his money?"

"Money is money."

Mezka went back to sitting silently and staring at the floor. Her shivering had died down, with only the occasional shake and shudder running up her spine. The man in the living armor stood straight and still, the vents along the side of his faceplate slowly opening and closing with each breath.

"When we find this man you are looking for, what will

you do with him?"

"The smart thing to do would be to give him to the man who paid me."

"And what will he do?"

The man in the living armor glanced out the window at the fluttering tarpaulin, the skittering sand. "I don't know. Anyway, I haven't decided whether I'll hand him over or not."

Mezka chewed on her lip.

"You object to what I do?"

Mezka kept on chewing.

"When I hired you to guide me here and speak to these people you didn't have any questions. Why ask them now?"

Mezka tried to show her indecision with her shoulders. The movement felt foreign to her. The man in the living armor hovered beside the window staring down at her. With his eyes hidden behind his faceplate Mezka could not read his expression. Even if she could, she was not sure she wanted to.

"The water seller, do you know him?"

Mezka lifted her hand and swiped it sideways.

"Does that mean No?"

Mezka balled up her fist and let it drop.

"Does that mean Yes?"

Mezka sighed. "Yes."

"Which is it?"

"I do not know this man, this water seller."

"He wasn't doing business when you were here last?"

"To be a water seller is a dangerous thing. Many people do not like to have to pay so much for water. In the Indusýra no one pays for their water. As long as they work everyone gets a share. Out here among the cacti it is different. You must pay."

The man in the living armor raised his fist and let it drop.

"You understand?"

"I understand."

Mezka adjusted her position, moving her legs under the sand. The left one had gone to sleep. As blood filtered back into her calf and foot, the leg began to tingle. She thought about rubbing it, but did not want the man in the living armor to see her discomfort.

"Sometimes the ones who sell the water are killed. Then someone else takes their place."

"Who was selling water when you were here last?"

Mezka dropped her head. "I do not know."

"You didn't buy water."

"Water was bought for me."

"By whom?"

"It was bought for me."

The man in the living armor turned and looked back out the window, his faceplate again catching the moonlight. Upon closer inspection Mezka thought it looked like the shell of a strange, talking insect. The armor was not black and glossy like the back of a beetle, instead it was sandy and rough like the back of a silt crawler.

"What happened to the people you were with, the ones who bought the water for you?"

"They died."

Again stepping from the rusted bar of the moonlight, the man in the living armor came and stood before Mezka. Slowly he lowered himself until he was squatting beside her. Reaching out he took hold of the water gourd he had purchased and pulled the stopper. Placing his knuckles against the mouth of the gourd, the man extended a thin length of carapace. Mezka heard the soft sound of water being siphoned from inside the gourd. After a moment the man replaced the stopper and withdrew the tendril.

"New plan: in the morning you and I will walk out of this settlement. We'll make it obvious which path we take and we'll make sure someone sees us. Once we're in the cactus we'll cut back to a spot where we can watch the gate. If the man I'm looking for comes out of the gate we'll be able to see him. If the water seller comes after us we'll be able to see him too."

Mezka lifted her fist and let it drop.

The man in the living armor nodded. "You should get some rest. Tomorrow—" He looked up sharply, turned towards the window.

Mezka stifled a yelp.

The man in the living armor crossed the room in a single stride. Pressing himself against the far wall he peered out the window. Mezka heard him suck in his breath. Extracting herself from the sand, she moved to stand beside him.

Tiny lights bobbed within the forest of cacti. As Mezka watched they began to emerge, first one, then another, and then another. Soon there were nine of them moving in single file. As they drew closer Mezka saw that each of the lights belonged to a man who sat perched upon a long-necked hýthric. Some of the men rode tall in the saddle, others were small and bent. One of them had two arms on his left side; another had a single horn growing from the middle of his forehead.

"Deviants."

The man in the living armor did not spit out the word like so many others would have. Instead he simply stated a fact. A moment later he stated another.

"This will not end well."

Four

Krýl watched them ride by, thirteen in all, smelling of sweat and hýthric. The conspicuous clank and rattle of the deviants' kit spoke of men who wanted to put on a show, veracity and vengeance on the hoof. Anyone serious about doing the settlement harm would have come without lights, their weapons and tack silenced. This was theatrics.

"They're not going to be pleased when they reach the bilaza."

The girl stood beside him staring wide-eyed as the last of the riders disappeared from view. Krýl put a hand on her shoulder. The girl jumped. Krýl took the hand away and gestured towards the door. "It would be best if you left now."

Krýl reached under his cloak and drew out three ingots. He held them out to the girl. She looked at his open palm, then back up at his faceplate. Gingerly she reached out and took the money.

Moving around the girl, Krýl poked his head out of the doorless entryway. There was no one in the street beyond, just a small plume of dust drifting in their direction. He managed three full steps before he heard the girl behind him.

When Krýl moved further into the jumble of sandstone buildings, the girl followed. He rounded a corner and the girl closed the distance between them. She kept to his left, six paces behind.

Krýl stopped and glanced over his shoulder. The girl stopped as well. "I said—"

From somewhere up ahead there came the sound of shouting. The shout was followed by a clatter of metal on stone and more raised voices. Krýl quickened his pace, slipping from one alley to another, following the clangor. Behind him the girl's breath came quick and heavy.

Ahead there was a light. Krýl rounded another corner and stopped. The girl nearly collided with him, drawing up at the last instant. Krýl turned to her. "When I said you should go, I meant you should go."

The girl lifted her hand and made her negating gesture.

"You brought me here," said Krýl. "You've been paid. Go on."

The tried shaking her head. She did so with vigor.

Krýl leaned forward so that his face was only inches from the girl's. "What happens next you do not want to get mixed up in."

The girl raised her chin. "You do not know what will happen."

From the direction of the light came another bout of shouting.

"I've got a pretty good idea."

"Then why would I leave and walk into the night?"

Krýl straightened and looked down at himself. "Being around me won't be safe. Not for a long while."

"It will not be safe for me to go."

Someone up ahead began screaming. It sounded thick and wet.

Krýl turned back towards the light. There was laughter and more screaming.

"Just stay out of sight."

Krýl did not hear what the girl said next; he was already striding into the light cast by the deviants' torches.

They had a man hung up by the heels, the skin of his chest cut lengthwise into ribbons. There was blood on his neck, his face, and the pavement below his head. He was doing his best to scream and keep from choking at the same time. The deviant working the man with a knife was not making it easy. It took a moment for Krýl to realize that the man dangling above the bloodied pavement was the cactus blossom seller.

Of the thirteen deviants, six had the graceful reptilian appearance Krýl had come to know and, in a small way, appreciate. The remaining seven were twisted things. They were afflicted with vestigial arms, extra eyes, perhaps the nub of a tail. Their skin was leathery, tinged red, orange, or speckled with yellow blotches that looked like caustic mold. Most had horns, though the puny things were bent and irregular. One, the largest of these seven, had been more fortunate. His limbs were proportionate, his back was straight, and a massive length of horn jutted from the middle of his forehead. He watched the cactus blossom seller through tiny black eyes nearly hidden beneath the tumid growth.

There was more cutting. The laughter swelled. The reptilian contingent clicked and chattered. Krýl stepped forward.

The deviants were intent on their fun, intent on watching the bloodied man wriggle and gasp. Krýl was inside their circle of torchlight before anyone took notice of him. When at last they did, the deviants fell silent. All eyes turned from the blossom seller to the armored interloper.

Krýl gestured to the hanging man. "You've nearly done for him."

The deviants glanced at the blossom seller, then back at Krýl. One of the reptilians opened its mouth and hissed. Even in the dime torchlight the pale flesh of its throat shone bright white.

The deviant with the horn stepped forward. He was tall, even without the growth jutting from the middle of his forehead. He raised one hand and pointed at Krýl with a riding crop. "Who the hell are you?"

"Krýl."

The horned deviant turned his head to one side—not

very much, but enough to angle the tip of his horn a good forty-five degrees. "What the hell is a Krýl?"

Krýl gestured towards the cactus blossom seller. The man had stopped his screaming and hung limp. He was still breathing, but the sound was forced and thin. "What did he do to deserve that?"

The horned deviant took another step. Krýl felt the armor draw tight around him. The beginnings of a blade crept out of his wrist accompanied by the familiar pang in the pit of his stomach. "What was his crime?"

"Crime?" the deviant turned his head the opposite direction producing another forty-five degree tilt with his horn.

"Or were you just having a bit of fun?"

Another of the reptilians hissed. Several of the rough-hewn deviants muttered and shuffled. Krýl kept his eyes on the one with the horn and let the symbiote worry about the rest.

"You see the cages?" The riding crop that had previously been directed at Krýl swept towards the five iron crow's nests.

Krýl nodded. "I saw them when I bought food from the man you've cut to shreds."

"Bones," said the horned deviant. "Deviant bones in the cages."

"He didn't put them there."

"He's human. He lives in the settlement."

Again Krýl nodded. "I'm human. Doesn't mean I put those deviants in those cages."

The horned deviant grinned. His teeth were a jumble of square slabs liked chipped blocks of granite.

Krýl felt the blade grow, inching past his knuckles.

"You? Human?" The horned deviant threw back his head and laughed. Several of the others tittered, but no one committed to outright guffaws.

"I'm looking for someone," said Krýl.

The laughter ceased and the horned deviant fixed him with an onyx-black stare.

Krýl lifted his left hand just above shoulder height. "He's about yay tall. Gold eyes. Odd complexion. Though I suppose that's relative. You'd know him if you'd seen him."

This time when the horned deviant showed his teeth it was not in a grin.

"Is that a yes?" asked Krýl. "He's worth a lot of money to me."

The horned deviant made a slashing gesture with his riding crop and bellowed. The hýthric standing in a cluster just outside the circle of torchlight shied and gurgled. Krýl felt the serrated length of carapace jump from the side of his right wrist. From the left a length of barbed tendril uncoiled itself.

Two of the deviants fell on him in tandem.

The man to Krýl's right died with an open throat, blood washing the cobbles. Where droplets of red touched the armor they disappeared, sucked beneath the surface. The deviant to Krýl's left died with the barbed tip of the tendril jutting from one eye. He went slack, hanging like so much charcuterie, propped up by the tendril. Krýl felt the armor begin to pull blood and cerebral fluid from the dead man.

There was silence, still and complete. It lasted for the span of five heartbeats. It was broken by the blossom seller taking one final, rasping breath.

Krýl lifted the body he had speared on the tendril, lifted it on the thin length of elastic carapace until its knees were dangling at head height. He then flung it at the feet of the horned deviant.

"You didn't just come here because these people take a

dim view of your kind."

The horned deviant blinked at Krýl. Krýl raised his left arm. The tendril lashed itself back and forth, then sunk into the back of the dead man and resumed shunting bits of him to the armor. Krýl could see it moving beneath the deviant's mottled skin, the corpse shifting and twitching. The remaining eleven deviants recoiled.

"You rode in after dark with torches," said Krýl, "did a bit of shouting, took a man and strung him up. You made a show of it."

The horned deviant's gaze flickered from the corpse, to Krýl, then back again.

"There's not enough of you to take the settlement and you didn't come for tea and fried cactus blossoms." Krýl cocked his own head to the side. "So why are you here?"

The horned deviant sneered. He pointed with his riding crop to the newly minted corpse and the tendril worming its way through the man's innards. "You are no human. You are no deviant. You are something worse."

The tendril began to work on the corpse's larger bones, cracking them open and sucking out the marrow. The symbiote's constant urging to be fed began to escalate.

"I'm human enough."

There was that sneer again, cracked lips working their way up and over blocky rows of teeth.

"Why are you and your men here?"

The horned deviant answered Krýl with a question of his own. "You are looking for a man, eh?"

"About yay tall." Krýl held up his hand, just above shoulder height.

"Gold eyes?"

"Gold eyes."

"What makes you think he be here?"

"I have it on good authority."

The horned deviant looked puzzled.

"Someone told me."

"Someone told us, too."

"Figured."

With a jerk, Krýl pulled the tendril from the corpse. The armor protested. He refocused its attention on the eleven other deviants standing around him in a semi-circle. Krýl felt the symbiote grow tense.

The horned deviant lifted his chin. "Why you want this man?"

"It's like I said," Krýl lifted his own chin, "he's worth a lot of money."

The horned deviant laughed. "Worth money!"

The others glanced at one another.

"You don't care about money?"

"More to life than money."

"Really?" Krýl took a step back; he couldn't help himself. "First time I've heard that."

"From a deviant?"

"From anyone."

"Man with gold eyes worth more than money."

"You don't say. To whom?"

"Do say." The horned deviant leaned forward. Krýl could see the flickering light from the torches dancing across the surface of his tiny black eyes. "Done talking. You go now."

"Go?"

The circle of deviants took a collective step forward. The tendril flicked left, flicked right, made a feint like a snake warding off a mongoose.

"You go," said the deviant again.

"No," said Krýl.

The horned deviant showed Krýl his teeth one last time,

big as bricks. "We let you walk out. We let you take your life and go. You say this No? Why?"

"The man you killed," Krýl gestured towards the body dangling from the crow's nest with his chest in tatters, "he made a damn good cactus blossom."

The horned deviant roared and slashed the air with his riding crop. Ten sets of eyes, ten blades, ten men fell on Krýl.

Five

Mezka screamed loud and long. The sound died in a sob and she shrank against the wall. The stones were rough on her cheek and on the palms of her hands. She pressed herself against them, tried to become a part of the narrow alley. She had only middling success.

Beyond her hiding place, Mezka's scream went unnoticed. There were too many other screams, too many roars, too many shouts. Mezka watched as the man in the living armor spitted one of the deviants on the blade he had grown from his wrist. When he withdrew the blade the deviant's bowels came with it. Mezka heard the wet splatter as loops of intestines struck the cobbles. When the tendril that grew from the man's other wrist punctured the skull of another deviant Mezka heard that too. The sound was like a gourd breaking.

The horned deviant bellowed and shoved the others towards the man in the living armor. They went with weapons raised only to be cut down, hacked, bludgeoned, and kicked. Two went down, then three, then four. A deviant with gnarled horns fell away clutching the stump of his arm, his face split wide in a silent scream.

Mezka felt her stomach do a somersault. She gagged,

clapped a hand over her mouth. The somersault came again and the cactus blossoms she had had for supper deposited themselves at her feet.

Coughing, choking, her eyes filling with tears and her hand wet with vomit, Mezka began to back down the alley. Her foot connected with a pile of refuse, old pottery and table scraps. The pile toppled, nearly taking Mezka with it. She steadied herself and wiped at the tears in her eyes.

The man in the living armor lashed the air with the tendril and charged the remaining deviants. They fell back bloodied, begging, hands held before them. The man in the living armor chopped at them as though they were cordwood. He threw the tattered remains aside, the tendril gouging off bits of flesh as he went. Then he was standing before the horned deviant.

From behind her, Mezka heard a stifled shout and a pattering of feet. She turned in time to see the men who were with the water seller. They had been halfway up the alley when the fighting broke out. Now they took to their heels. The water seller followed after, the flame of his torch streaming out behind him.

The horned deviant bellowed. Mezka turned herself around as the man in the living armor caught the deviant's horn in the chest. He went sprawling, legs in the air. The horned deviant bellowed again and set his feet for another charge.

Landing on his back, the man in the living armor used his momentum to turn himself upright. Tucking his feet under him, he sprang at the horned deviant. They met with a crash, the man slashing at the deviant amidst a riot of roaring and shaking.

Mezka felt the alley begin to tilt. She put out a hand, bracing herself against the wall. More tears welled up in her eyes turning the world into a liquid blur of gray and flickering orange. Her knees buckled and her legs went out from under her. Sliding down the rough wall, Mezka slumped amidst the rubbish.

There was another crash, a wet thump, then all was quiet. The wind puffed, bringing with it the smell of spilled blood and burned pitch.

Mezka looked up. She wiped the tears from her eyes. The alley walls blocked most of her view, but what she could see of the square was littered with bodies. The remains of the deviants were strewn about in a hacked and bloody shambles, piled one atop the other. The torches they had carried lay scattered and sputtering. In their waning light Mezka could see a thin rivulet of blood winding its way slowly in her direction. Mezka recoiled and tried to get to her feet. This proved more difficult than expected and she slumped back down, scraping her palms.

It was then that the man in the living armor came striding out of the dying torchlight, the upper half of the horned deviant scraping along behind him. When he reached the spot where Mezka had fallen, he stopped. Reaching down, he took her by the arm. Mezka took it back.

"We should go."

"You—"

"Killed them? I did."

"How—"

"Could I? Quite easily."

Between the man's legs Mezka could see the bifurcated remains of the horned deviant. Death had done little to change the expression on his face. He still stared out at the world through beady black eyes, his lips drawn back over the stony blocks of his teeth.

The man in the living armor saw her looking. "Don't

mind him. I doubt he'll be any more trouble."

Mezka watched the tendril buried in the deviant's chest scrape, and cut, and suck. With an effort she tore her eyes away and fixed them on the man in the living armor. He knelt down and extended his hand.

"Come."

Mezka shook her head.

"You were the one who wouldn't stay put. You were the one who followed me here. Now you want to stay huddled in an alley filled with garbage?"

Mezka glared.

"This place is about to become very unpleasant for you and me. I suggest we follow the advice you gave earlier and take our leave."

Mezka looked around the alley, at the fading glow of the torches, back at the man in the living armor. Behind him the tendril continued to work at the carcass of the deviant.

"Make it stop."

The man glanced over his shoulder. "The armor's going to keep at it until it's satisfied or we get up and go."

Mezka made a face.

"It won't pay any attention to you, not since it's been fed."

"You promise this thing?"

The man moved his head up and down.

"Say it."

"I promise." The man turned his hand palm up. "My name is Krýl."

Mezka put her hand in his. "Mezka."

THE HARDPAN

One

The man in the living armor, the man who called himself
Krýl, sat on his hýthric as though he had been born to the
saddle. He rolled with each gangly stride, the reins held casu-
ally in one hand. The animal had stopped trying to throw
him after the first two hours and now he rode with one leg
cocked over the saddle horn. Mezka had not been so lucky.
Less than an hour ago her hýthric had tried to rub her off
on a grove of cacti. It was all Mezka could do to keep from
being skewered. After that Krýl had taken her reins and tied
them to his saddle. This had quelled the worst of the hýthric's
behavior, but it continued to give her baleful glances over its
shoulder.

The pack animal that had been tied to Krýl's saddle
was now strapped to Mezka's, turning them into a caravan
in miniature. Together they moved single file through low,

rocky hills and fell groves of cacti. Overhead the sun hung bloated and red, the sky the color of burnished copper. The wind blew in sporadic gusts out of the east, hazing the horizon and sending dust devils whirling in the distance. The monotony of rust-colored stones and wind-blown grit was offset only by the green of the cacti, the orange of their blossoms, the glint of their spines.

Krýl made a clicking sound with his tongue and tapped his mount with his riding crop. The hýthric swung its long neck to the left and angled itself between two stands of cacti. As they passed through the patchy shadows beneath the towering cladodes, Mezka unstoppered her water and drank. She then drank again. Behind her she heard the slosh of the water gourds strapped to the back of the pack animal. There were seven of them, more than enough. She had another drink.

"Go easy."

Krýl did not turn as he spoke. He kept his eyes on the way ahead, touched the flank of his hýthric with his riding crop.

Mezka opened her mouth to reply, then shut it again.

Krýl turned and looked at her out of the corner of one eye. It was his own eye, the armored faceplate having peeled itself off and tucked itself away. His bald head was now covered by the tattered hood of his cloak.

"Speak."

Mezka cleared her throat.

"After all that water you must have spit enough to speak, so speak."

Mezka tugged part of her robe over her mouth and nose. "Those men, the deviants…"

The man in the living armor nodded. "What about them?"

"Why did you…" Mezka paused, thinking of black blood

reflecting torchlight and dead eyes staring at nothing. She shook her head and looked away

The man in the living armor shrugged and looked away. He patted his hýthric with the riding crop.

Mezka was unsure how long it took the words to come, but when they did they tumbled off of her tongue like rubies through a Shah's fingers. "Why did you kill all of those men? The last of them tried to give up or run, but you would not let them go. You cut at them until there was nothing left."

Krýl continued to look straight ahead, his body rolling with the movement of the hýthric.

Mezka pressed her lips tightly together and looked off towards a stand of cacti. They looked much the same as the last stand, and the stand before that.

Krýl coughed, cleared his throat. "Kill one man and you've made an enemy of his friends. Kill them all and you've got no enemies left." He paused for a moment. "Besides, we needed their hýthric and their water."

Mezka watched the cacti slide past. The wind made them sway, if only a little. By contrast, her robe fluttered around her like a pennon, pressing against her thin frame.

Krýl turned in his saddle to regard her. Mezka did not take her eyes from the cacti.

"You can leave any time you like."

Mezka's head snapped around. Through the saddle she felt her hýthric start and shy to one side.

"I said as much back in the settlement." Krýl waved a hand over his shoulder. "I'll chase down my bounty on my own."

One of the hýthric brayed. Mezka crossed her arms and put her nose in the air.

Krýl again turned to look at her. "Any time you like."

"No," said Mezka.

"No?"

"It is as I have said."

"Suit yourself."

In the silence that followed the wind picked itself up and sent a dust devil pirouetting across their path. Krýl slowed the hýthric to let it pass.

"What if I gave you half of the water? You would have that, the money I paid you, and a hýthric."

Mezka narrowed her eyes and peered at the back of Krýl's head. Beneath his hood she was sure he was chuckling to himself.

"Well?"

"Do not make fun of me."

"I'm not making fun of you."

"Then why do you offer me half of the water?"

"What do you mean why?"

"This I have already said as well." Mezka could feel heat rising in her cheeks. She raised a hand, discovered the hem of her robe had slipped down, and pulled it back over her mouth and nose.

"I offered you half of the water because you're obviously not thrilled with the prospect of being dragged along in my wake."

"What is a wake?"

"Dragged along behind me."

Mezka narrowed her eyes as another gust blew by.

"Back in the settlement, when I pulled you out of that alley, you could hardly stand and you'd been sick all over your feet. You've put yourself together, faster than some soldiers I've known. Since then I've shared the water and kept your hýthric from perforating you. And yet you still think I might do the same thing to you that I did to those deviants. Tell me I'm wrong."

Mezka clenched her jaw and pressed her lips into a thin line.

"Tell me I'm wrong," said the man in the living armor.

"You are not wrong."

He turned to look at her again. His brow and bald head were in shadow, the dust-streaked patch of beard that clung to his jaw the only thing visible beneath his hood. "I have no intention of cutting you up and letting this thing," he held up one armored hand, "have a go at you. To prove as much I'm offering to let you go."

Mezka scoffed. "You are offering to let me go to my death."

Krýl raised his head and Mezka could see that his brow was furrowed. "How so?"

"A woman alone on the sand with money and water… what do you think I mean?"

"There's no one else out here."

"No, not out here! But there will be people at the next settlement. What happens to me when I ride up to their gate? The Kommhadi will say that I stole the hýthric and the water. They will take my money and they will put me in a cell. When they are done raping me they will sell me as a slave. Or maybe they will just hang me."

Krýl looked off in the direction of the cacti. He did not speak for a long time. Mezka adjusted her weight in the saddle, trying to work some life into her backside. She had not realized how painful sitting in a saddle could be.

"Better to ride with me than face the open desert and the next settlement alone, is that it?" Krýl tapped his mount with the riding crop. It shook its horned head, but straightened itself out.

Mezka raised her voice; she spoke as clearly as she could manage. "You will not find the man you are chasing without me. You do not know this place, not like I do."

"Alright then," said Krýl. "How much further to Dhul-kant?"

Mezka felt herself uncoil and she sagged in the saddle. Her hýthric made a gurgling sound deep in its throat. Krýl sat at ease, his own hýthric swishing its tail back and forth, waiting for her to respond.

"If we keep in this direction we will pass it on our right in five days." Mezka pointed to the northeast. "If we go that direction we will reach the city in four and a half days."

Krýl smiled, tugged at his beard, and pointed to the northeast. "Then we shall go that way."

Two

Krýl watched the sky from behind the angular redoubt of his faceplate. Around him the wind was an angry dervish that sent dust skyward in great columns. Seen through this moving veil, the sun looked to Krýl like a flat disk of metal pulled from a forge. Long shadows stretched away from the surrounding cacti, shifting as they swayed and knocked into one another.

Beside him, Mezka stood with the reins of their hýthric clutched in one small fist. She had her other hand planted on the top of her head, pressing the hood of her robe down against her skull. Her eyes were shut against the blowing sand.

"We can't stay the night out in the open."

The girl peeked at Krýl from beneath her hood.

"We can't stay the night in the cactus either."

The girl closed her eyes and braced herself as the wind redoubled its efforts. Krýl braced himself as well, his already tattered cloak fraying itself against the surface of the armor.

The hýthric sat with their legs tucked beneath them, faces turned from the wind, nictitating membranes hiding their eyes.

The sun hovered just above a low cluster of hills silhouetted against its burning flank.

"There." Krýl pointed.

The girl opened her eyes and squinted into the distance. "No."

"Why not?"

"Ruins are not a place for the living."

Krýl looked at the girl, then back at the jumble of cut stones and half-tumbled walls perhaps a mile distant. "Ruins are just stone and memories. They can be a lifesaver if you happen to be caught in a sandstorm…or worse."

"Worse?"

"Crystal."

The girl tried to make her negating gesture with the hand holding her hood in place. The result was a bare head and tousled hair. When she had her hood back in place she said, "No crystal here. We are too far to the south and the west."

"Tell that to the simians."

"To the what?"

"Nothing. Come." Krýl had to raise his voice to be heard over the wind.

The girl tried shaking her head in response.

"Would you rather spend the night out here?"

"Not in the ruins."

"Why?"

"Ruins are not a place for the living."

"So you've said." Krýl tried to keep his annoyance out of his voice. "You want to wander around in the cactus until we find someplace to bed down? The wind has turned them into a gauntlet of knives."

The girl pointed to a stand of cacti off to the east. "They are far enough apart and the wind will not last all night."

"How can you be certain?"

"The wind will not last."

Krýl chewed his lip. "Fine."

Taking the reins from the Mezka's hand, Krýl tapped the lead hýthric with his riding crop, prodding it back to its feet. It complied, though not without a groan of protest. He then turned the small caravan in the direction of the cacti.

The moon was high when the wind finally died. By its light the girl went hunting amongst the cacti for dried pads. These she piled in the middle of the sandy patch they had discovered after ducking and weaving their way through the swaying cladodes. When she had a sizable pile, Mezka took flint and steel from the pouch she kept hidden in her robes and struck a spark. She then bent low and blew on the tiny flame until it could breathe on its own.

Krýl watched Mezka settle herself by the fire, one leg crossed over the other. From her hýthric's saddlebags she produced a bowl and filled it with dried bits of something brown. Krýl's nose wrinkled when he caught its scent. The symbiote told him not to touch it, whatever it was.

"How did you know the wind would die down?"

Mezka fished one of the brown bits from the bowl and popped it into her mouth. She made a sour face, then began to chew. When she had swallowed she said, "It is always this way at this time of year. The wind blows a little in the morning, more in the afternoon, much at sunset. By moonrise it has begun to die away."

"What causes it, do you know?"

The girl made a gesture with her hand.

"So, you don't know?"

"It is the way of things."

Mezka reached out and gently placed another dried cactus pad on the fire. Krýl watched it catch then said, "Why the fire? You're not cooking anything and there isn't enough fuel for more than an hour or two."

Mezka looked at him, then up at the shadows dancing amongst the cacti. "It is good to have a friend."

"A friend?"

Mezka bobbed her fist once, then took another morsel from the bowl. This one went down with another grimace and a swallow from one of the water gourds.

"What is that?"

"I do not know."

"If it came from a deviant's saddlebag I'm not sure I would eat it."

"Then what shall I eat?"

Krýl looked around, shrugged. "You've got a point."

Another morsel and another grimace. "You are not hungry?"

"No."

Mezka watched him for a time, smoke curling between them. "That is good. I do not want to share."

Krýl chuckled.

A stray gust of wind sent a thread of sand skittering across the open space where they had made camp. For a moment the flames gnawing at the cactus pads turned blue and threatened to go out. When the wind died they sprang up again, yellow-orange like the cactus blossoms.

"Why did you pick me?"

The question took Krýl unawares. His scratched at his temple, lifted an eyebrow, asked, "What do you mean?"

Mezka took another drink from the water gourd. "You could have chosen any one of the guides in Mahul to take you through the cacti. Why did you pick me?"

Krýl thought for a moment. "Because the others looked like they wanted to kill me or run from me. You stood your ground and looked me in the eye."

"Most men would have taken that as an insult."

Krýl raised a gauntleted hand and spread his fingers. "I am not most men."

Mezka ate and drank, taking her time, chewing slowly. She fed the fire again, prodded its edges with her stick.

"Were you always a guide?"

"No."

"Then what were you?"

"I was a slave."

Krýl sat up straighter. "A slave?"

Mezka bobbed her fist up and down. "Raiders took me when I was eleven. I lived with the Shásh for a year, with their women. After I started to bleed they took me to a market, put me on an auction block, and accepted bids for me. A merchant bought me, a man with a round face and a white beard. I served him for a time. Then I was free."

"After the merchant you weren't sold to another."

The girl made the swiping motion with her hand.

"Were you a concubine?"

Again Mezka made the swiping motion. "I spoke for my master when men from far off places came to his house. Language comes to me better than it does to others. I would be his tongue when he traded, or bought, or sold. I travelled with him for many months out of the year."

Krýl waited for the girl to go on. She tugged at the hem of her robe and tried to unstick her tongue from the roof of her mouth. He could see her pulse beating along the side of her throat. Through the armor he could smell the sweat that beaded her forehead.

"He died, fell out of his saddle. It was very hot. He lay on the ground, his face red, his eyes rolled up to the whites. The guards and the other slaves took what they wanted and left. I waited until they were gone, then took the water the others could not carry and I left too."

Krýl looked down at the ground, then back at the girl. The fire popped, sending up a small shower of sparks.

Mezka put a hand to her chest and took a deep breath. Krýl watched the throbbing of her pulse slow, felt the armor stir, and then settle back into place. Mezka reached into her bowl, picked out something red, and ate it. As she hastily chewed and swallowed, she gestured to Krýl. "The armor—tell me."

"Tell you what?"

"Tell me, does it think?"

"In its own way."

"Where did it come from?"

"I don't know."

"Does it belong to you, or do you belong to it?"

"I don't know."

The girl made a face. "Then where did you get it?"

"I found it in a cave."

"A cave?" asked the girl. She made another face, her brow furrowed.

"The cave was deep in the desert; the armor was deep in the cave."

"Then how did you find it?"

"I was looking for water."

Mezka bobbed her fist and her expression softened. After a moment she said, "It is alive."

"Is that a question?"

"No. I have seen it move on its own."

"You've seen it do more than that."

Mezka bobbed her fist again. "It eats."

Krýl got up from his place by the fire and sat down beside her. When the girl stiffened he scooted a few inches further away. Krýl raised his left arm. Tentatively the girl raised her hand, reached out, then drew her fingers back again. Krýl chuckled.

"The thing that came out of this arm, the thing that looks like a whip, that's how the armor eats. There used to be a dozen of them. Came from here," he gestured to a place between his shoulder blades, "but not anymore."

"What happened?"

Krýl lowered his head. "Cut away, the ends blackened."

"Fire?"

"Poison."

Mezka thought for a moment. "Who cut them?"

Krýl shook his head. "Doesn't matter. I only need the one."

"Are you worried about more poison?"

"There's no way that I know of to make more of the stuff. There was a fire."

Mezka's lips turned themselves up in a half smile. "I knew there would be a fire."

"War is full of it."

Mezka bobbed her fist, then turned her palm up, opened her fingers and closed them again.

"What does that mean?"

"It means a question."

"Ask."

"It means a question that might offend."

"Doubtful."

The girl regarded Krýl. "You are strange."

"Why? Because I walk around in a suit of armor that kills men and eats them, or because I don't offend easily?"

"Strange," said the girl. For a moment the smile flickered back to life.

"Well, what's your question?"

Mezka cleared her throat. "The armor ate the deviants that came to the settlement. The armor is a part of you. Does this mean you ate those deviants as well?"

Krýl lowered his head and sucked an incisor. He prodded the sand with a carapaced toe. "I suppose it does."

The girl wrapped her arms around herself and leaned towards the fire.

In the distance, something called out, its voice dry as dust. Krýl looked up at the faded patch of stars just visible between the cacti. In the glow of the fire he saw his breath billow like smoke. When he looked down again the girl had begun to heap handfuls of sand onto the fire. It died with a red flicker and a hiss.

Reaching to his throat, Krýl unbuckled his cloak and held it out to the girl.

"No."

"Take it, the night's gone cold."

"No," said the girl again, "I do not need it."

Krýl heard a rustle of leather and fabric, the clink of buckles. The girl pulled one heavy blanket from her saddle-bags, then another. She wrapped them around her shoulders, turned her back to him, and lay down.

For a while Krýl sat listening, the darkness around him filled with the whisper of the wind and the faint creak of the cacti. Crossing his legs, Krýl propped his hands on his knees. He watched the ball of blankets that was Mezka for a moment. She did not stir.

Krýl smiled. "I'll take the first watch then, shall I?"

Three

"I can see two of them." The girl, shading her eyes with one hand, squinted up at the sky. "No, three of them."

Krýl felt the symbiote tense. Along his back, a row of spines began to press against the nearly threadbare fabric of his cloak.

"Yes," said Mezka, "there are three." She pointed towards the horizon.

Shading his own eyes, Krýl glared in the direction of the three specks. They moved in languid circles, riding the thermals, their wings canted. "Fucking vermin."

Mezka lowered her hand and peered at Krýl out of one eye. The other was squeezed tightly shut against blowing sand and the glare of the sun. "They do not look like vermin to me. They are much bigger than rats."

"Trust me, they're vermin."

"Why do you say this thing?"

"Spend enough time on a battlefield after the killing's done and you'll understand."

"That is not something I want to understand."

Krýl sniffed. "You're better for it."

The shapes rose higher, their circle widening. Krýl could just make out the glint of sunlight on the crowns of their heads.

"This way?" asked Mezka, pointing with her chin. "Or this way?"

Krýl looked to the north and west. Both directions were filled to overflowing with cacti. To either side walls of decaying sandstone blocked their path. Somehow they had managed to funnel themselves into a trench. The cladodes ahead were no higher than a man, but their spines were long, and thin, and white. Unlike the other stands of cacti, these were dark green and covered with violet blotches. Krýl thought they looked surly and liable to bite.

Mezka saw him glaring at the local flora and said, "Glass thorns."

"Thorns?" Krýl glanced at her. "Those are cactus; cactus have spines."

"I did not name them."

Krýl shrugged. "Why do they call them glass thorns?"

"Why do you think?"

Turning in his saddle, Krýl looked back the way they had come. He rubbed one wrist across his forehead and contemplated spitting. He decided not to waste the moisture.

"I am sorry," said Mezka. "I have not been here before. Each time I came this way my master had us walking the hardpan."

"It's not your fault. I should've known better. Going around would've taken longer, but there's a reason the caravan routes avoid…this." Krýl gestured to the sandstone and the cacti.

In the distance the shapes wheeled higher still, their wings dark blotches against the sun.

Krýl tugged the reins, pulling his hýthric around until it was facing south. Mezka's mount and the animal carrying their water followed. After a few dozen yards Mezka nudged her hýthric alongside his own.

"Five miles back," said Krýl, "maybe more. This nonsense will take us the better part of the morning. After that…well, you tell me."

Mezka pointed eastward. "After that the land is flat. It is cracked and hot. There is a road, but it is not such a good road. Sometimes it disappears; sometimes it leads in the wrong direction. Best to just go in the way you need to go and not pay much attention to it."

"The road leads in the wrong direction? How does it manage that?"

Mezka made a back and forth gesture with her hand. "I do not know the answer to this."

"Is it the sand?" asked Krýl.

"It is on the hardpan. There is little sand."

"Then how?"

Mezka shrugged. The gesture was clunky and exaggerated.

Krýl chuckled. "And after the hardpan?"

Mezka stiffened. "Are you laughing at me?"

"No."

"You laughed. You laughed at me."

"No," said Krýl solemnly, "I would never do such a thing."

The girl narrowed her eyes. "You would do such a thing. You have just done it. Tell me why?"

Krýl tried to keep a smile from lips. "You shrugged."

"Shrugged?"

"The thing you did with your shoulders. It's called a shrug."

"That is a strange word for it, shrug."

"It's a strange thing to do, I guess. Seems appropriate though, gets the point across."

"It means that you do not know a thing," said Mezka, her tone matter-of-fact.

"Correct." Krýl bobbed his fist.

Mezka smiled. Krýl could see it in her eyes, above the swatch of robe that was wrapped around her mouth and nose. Those eyes were very dark.

Krýl lifted his hand and bobbed it up and down again. "Is this a Kommhadi thing to do?"

Mezka turned her head left, right, left again. "It is done

by everyone in the deep desert."

"Not everyone."

"Yes," said the girl, "everyone."

"I've been in plenty of deep deserts and can't recall ever seeing it before."

"That does not make sense."

"Oh?" Krýl cocked his head to one side.

"When you are in the deep desert and covered from head to foot in a robe to protect you from the sun it only makes sense to use the hand to speak with."

Krýl thought about this for a moment. "I suppose there's an argument to be made for a quaint little custom like that."

"Quaint?" Mezka made an abrupt gesture Krýl had not seen before. "It is the only custom that makes sense!"

"I've ridden a hundred deserts with a hundred different kinds of people and none of them have used this little language of yours."

Mezka stiffened. "Then the world is full of barbarians and fools."

The sandstone ridge they had been following, the one that had led them so adroitly into the wall of glass thorns, had begun to taper and widen. On its weather-worn surface Krýl could see scattered pebbles and crumbling cleavage. The eyes of a lizard stared out from a crevasse made by two sedimentary layers that had begun to peel away from one another.

"You're not wrong."

Mezka raised her head imperiously. "I know that I am not wrong."

For a time, they rode in silence listening to the wind sigh and the hýthric's tack jingle and clank. At last Krýl said, "It's a good custom. There's a certain logic to it."

"I know that too." The girl's chin remained high.

"Though there is—"

If Krýl had blinked he would have missed the first shadow to flicker across the sandstone. The second was there and gone almost as quickly. Krýl snapped his head up, burying his face in the hood of his cloak and blocking his line of sight. Tugging the fabric from his head, he squinted at the sky. "Fucking vermin."

Mezka screamed.

Krýl jerked sideways as a dark shape cut between his mount and the girl's. She screamed again as her hýthric bolted.

Still attached to Krýl's saddle by its reins, the panicked hýthric made it only far enough to unseat him. Krýl tumbled sideways, striking the ground with his shoulder. Before his heels touched the dirt the armor had risen to cover his head and face. Through yellowed membranes he watched as another black shape fell from the sky and attached itself to the back of the pack animal. The air was suddenly filled with the sound of flapping wings and clacking beaks.

Pulling himself to his feet, Krýl unlimbered the feeding tendril. It came reluctantly. Krýl snapped his wrist to the side and forced the tendril loose. He managed two full steps before something struck him in the back, bowling him over.

Through rising dust and rearing hýthric, Krýl made an attempt to roll first left, then right. The weight pinning him to the ground kept him where he was, face pressed against the cracked earth. When he again tried to shift his weight, the thing on top of him bit his head.

This time the symbiote did not quail or hesitate. It lashed out with the tendril—a blur of barbed exoskeleton that splashed red blood and black feathers across Krýl's field of vision. The weight lifted, if only slightly. Tucking his legs under him and burying his knuckles in the dust, Krýl heaved.

He came upright amidst a torrent of flapping and squalling.

"Fucking vermin!"

They had heads like skulls, a grotesque amalgamation of tendons and connective tissue layered over what appeared to be bare bone. Krýl knew from experience it had more in common with armor plating. Below the crests of their heads were beaks like scimitars, long and sharp. Around their necks was a ruff of white feathers; the rest were black as pitch. Had they bothered to stand still rather than jump, flap, and rake the air with their talons, they would have been nearly as tall as Krýl himself.

Moving about as they were, it was nearly impossible to draw a bead on any single bird. Even the one the armor had cut was again beating the air overhead with wings wide enough to blot out the sun. Krýl watched it rise, then fall, harrowing the two hýthric still standing, beads of blood glistening in its feathers.

"Fucking! Vermin!"

Krýl set his feet, drew back the barbed tendril, and whipped it around in a great arch. He cut the feet from the nearest bird, the thing screeching and flapping higher even as its talons fell to earth. Krýl drew back the tendril for another swing, managed to cock his arm forward, and was hit again. This time the force of the impact drove him forward, his back bowed, his arms and legs spread to the side. He knocked into one of the rearing hýthric, rebounded, and wound up crouched in the dust.

The girl screamed. The hýthric screamed. The birds screamed. Krýl felt as though he were in an echo chamber, one filled with constant motion, a dizzying blur of living shadows and searing light. For a single fleeting moment he considered letting the armor take control, letting it lash out at anything and everything, misting the hot air with blood.

He let the thought pass.

The second hýthric to fall was his own. Krýl watched it go down, legs flailing, throat open. Armored heads and rending beaks began taking it apart even before it ceased its thrashing. That left only Mezka and her animal.

Krýl bolted.

Ducking a strike from the bird whose legs he had cut away, Krýl leapt for the girl's hýthric. Jamming his knee into Mezka's saddle horn, Krýl propelled himself up and away from the terrified animal. In midair he clutched at the nearest black shape, wrapping his arms around one pulsing wing and the thing's armoured neck. His weight dragged it down, dropping it like a stone.

They hit the ground at the same time, Krýl and the bird. The armor took the shock of the impact, cushioning his fall. The bird broke. Its wings crumpled, its ribs caved, its back snapped. The armored head bounced off the crumbling sandstone, turned itself almost all the way around, and flopped back down.

Krýl scrambled away from the carcass, kicking it as he went. His backward progress nearly took him into the path of Mezka's hýthric. Krýl rolled to the side just in time to let it pass. When he looked up, he saw its retreating haunches half obscured by a cloud of rising dust. Quick on its trail was another black shape, wings spread like a funeral shroud in flight.

Whipping the tendril around, Krýl aimed as best he could for the hurtling bird and managed to cut away most of its left wing. The bird flapped once and went careening off to the side.

Krýl got to his feet. Raising his head, the lenses over his eyes darkening as he looked skyward, he hunted for the third shape, the bird whose legs lay a half dozen yards away. After a moment he saw it rising, trying for one of the thermals boiling up from the distant hardpan. It nearly made it.

Tilting to one side, the bird began to fall. It flapped awkwardly, tried for a lopsided glide, then fell towards the glass thorns. Krýl watched it disappear into the brittle wall of spines.

Mezka could not stop shaking. Krýl's efforts at comforting her produced no result. So, he left her where she was, arms wrapped around her knees, eyes fixed on absolutely nothing.

The hýthric was another story. It had a gash down one shoulder and half of an ear had been bitten away. In contrast to the girl's mute withdrawal, the hýthric was mad as hell and intent on making its feelings known. Krýl tried calming the animal so he could examine its injuries, but the symbiote was still too volatile. The hýthric sensed the armor's desire and decided Krýl was no longer welcome near it. He received a kick to the knee before he finally put up his hands and stepped away.

That left the birds. There were two of them lying perhaps a hundred paces apart. The evidence of their malfeasance was strewn about in the form of pulverized sandstone, fans of blood, and the carcasses of two good hýthric. Krýl cursed them a dozen times, then once more for good measure.

The pack animal had gotten the worst of it. All three of the birds had laid into the poor beast with beak and claw. The added effect of this savaging had been the near complete loss of their water. Not the flasks strapped to their mounts, fortunately, but every spare drop they had taken from the deviants had soaked into the ground or been taken by the sun. The only thing to have benefited from this fiasco was the armor. Since there was no sense in wasting good meat,

Krýl let it gorge itself on the fallen hýthric.

Leaning to one side, Mezka braced herself on her palms and made gagging noises. Krýl stepped her way, one hand outstretched. "No, no, no, don't do that."

Mezka made another gagging noise, then looked up at him. Her dark eyes were bloodshot and puffy from crying.

"Vomit and you lose water."

Mezka's expression changed to something between a frown and a sneer.

"The water is mostly gone." Krýl tapped his chest. "This thing will keep me alive, but you need every drop that's left."

Mezka went very pale. She had seen men die of thirst. The thought of going out the same way was a sobering one.

"Sit up," said Krýl.

Mezka sat up.

"Take a deep breath."

Mezka took a deep breath.

"Look at me."

Mezka looked at him. Krýl nodded.

"You'll be alright."

Turning about, Krýl stalked to where the carcass of the first bird lay, its reduced wing sticking straight up, its pin feathers fluttering in the breeze. He could feel Mezka's eyes on him as he bent down and cupped the thing's head in his hands.

Its eyes were glassy, tiny beads that stared out from beneath a low bony crest. The beak was half open, its barbed tongue just barely visible. Krýl flicked the side of bird's jaw and gave a satisfied snort when its beak clacked shut.

"Nice try, but I've seen that trick before."

Drawing on the fresh supply of meat and offal the armor had crammed into itself, Krýl extended a blade from his right wrist. He then palmed the bird's head in one hand and used the blade to hack at the overlapping plates of bone that ran along the back of its neck. When at last the head came free, Krýl lifted it. He stared into its reassuringly dead eyes and snorted.

"How do you like that, hm?"

The bird's jaw relaxed and its mouth fell open. The armor told Krýl to put the head back where he had found it. Krýl tucked it into a fold of his cloak instead. He then repeated the process with the second bird. When that was done he made his way to where Mezka sat with her legs crossed and her hands on her knees. He took a seat beside her and dumped the heads at her feet.

Mezka looked at the skulls, then back at Krýl. "Why?"

"I thought you might like a trophy or two. Not everyone can say they've seen one of these bastards up close and lived to tell about it."

"You are making a joke."

"I am."

"Do not make any more."

Krýl regarded the girl. "Too soon?"

Mezka did not respond, just sat and stared at the nearly skeletal remains of the two hýthric.

"The armor's very thorough. Waste not, want not."

Mezka lifted her hand and bobbed it once. She turned to Krýl and again said, "Why?"

"Why what?"

"Why did they…" she waved in the direction of the birds, the hýthric, the broken and bloodied sandstone.

"Why did they attack us?" Krýl thought for a moment. "I've been trying to figure that out myself."

Mezka blinked at him. Krýl looked down at the two heads lying in the dirt.

"I've seen them peck a wounded man to death. I've seen them swarm an injured hýthric. I've seen them pull apart a man that was too weak from lack of water to even crawl. But I've never seen them fall from the sky and tear two healthy animals to bits."

"This does not comfort me."

"Nor should it."

Reaching down, Krýl picked up the two skulls. He turned them in his hands, their glassy eyes seeming to follow him.

"What are you planning to do with those?"

Krýl set one of the skulls back on the ground. Extending a thin rod of chitin from his index finger, he poked it through one eye and out the other. He held up the skull and peered through the hole he had made. On the other side was a pin-prick image of Mezka. Krýl gave the second skull the same treatment, then reached into the folds of his cloak and brought out a piece of cord. This he strung through the two skulls, knotting it on either side to keep them from sliding back and forth. When he was satisfied they were not going anywhere he presented the dangling heads to Mezka. She gagged and put her hand to her mouth.

"Come now, it's bad manners to refuse a gift."

Mezka swiped her fist from side to side. Krýl tossed the heads in her lap.

"Stay right there, I'll get some feathers to tie on the end of your stick."

Mezka pushed the heads into the dust.

Krýl returned with a handful of feathers and more cord, thin and made of braided gut. This he wound around the end of Mezka's stick, inserting the long black feathers as he went. He handed it to her when he was finished and again reached for the skulls.

"These," said Krýl, giving the two heads a shake, "are

damned difficult to come by."

Mezka examined her stick. The feathers fluttered in the wind, vane and bard still sticky with blood. It looked as though she wanted to cast it from her.

"I do not care that they are difficult to come by."

"They may be vermin, but they're still feared."

"So?"

"So, how do you think people will look at you if you wear a pair of skulls around your waist and a clutch of feathers on your stick?"

Mezka scrunched up her forehead.

Krýl let the skulls dangle from the barbed point of his index finger. "They'll look at you with caution. They'll think twice about trying to take your water."

Mezka hesitated for a moment, then reached out and took the length of cord. With a frown tugging at the corners of her mouth, she looped it around her waist and tied it. When she was done the skulls hung at her left hip.

Krýl got to his feet and held out his hand. After a moment Mezka took it. When she was standing beside him, Krýl gestured to their one remaining hýthric. "You'll have to be the one to look after him. Wise fellow that he is, he won't let me near him."

"It is alright," said the girl, "I have attended hýthric before."

It took an hour and then some to calm the animal and stitch its shoulder. By the time they were again on the move and following their own backtrail, the sun had begun to slip towards the west. Their shadows spread out to the side, looking like a strange beast with eight legs, three heads, and carrying a feathered stick.

Four

On the hardpan, the wind was constant and strong. It blew out of the east, driving before it waves of sand from distant dunes. The sand rose in great plumes that turned the sky a sickly shade that reminded Mezka of old ivory. When the sun deigned to show itself, it appeared flat and dun.

Holding the neck of her robe closed with one hand, Mezka grasped the tether of the hýthric with the other. She pulled the protesting animal along, stepping carefully over baked earth split into a lattice of overlapping cracks. For as far as she could see in every direction, the land was as sheer and hot as a scudder's blade. Behind her, the man in the living armor trudged with his face covered by carapace and the hood of his cloak pulled low. All Mezka could see of him was his chin and the flash of the membranes over his eyes. When the sand had first begun to blow, he had offered her his cloak, but she had refused. If she had felt the need, she could have wrapped herself in one of the blankets from the hýthric's saddlebags. Mezka did not want the blankets, nor did she want the offered cloak. She wanted to be some-where—anywhere—else.

Overhead the sky grew alternately dark, then light, then dark again. As the sand rolled by it obscured the road, then again laid it bare. Each step was a journey unto itself, a fight against the wind, the dust, the potential loss of the road.

"There!"

The word was snatched by the wind and carried past her ear at a gallop. Mezka turned towards Krýl. He was point-ing off to the right, at a dark shape barely visible amidst the shifting and erratic light.

Mezka raised her fist and swiped it sideways. Krýl pointed again and started towards the mound. For a moment Mezka hesitated. Around her the swirling sand rose and fell; the wind howled. She looked up at the sun, then back at Krýl. She sighed and pulled at the hýthric's reins. It resisted. Tucking her right foot against her knee, she instead leaned against the great smelly beast. Ahead of her, Krýl hunkered by the mound, prodding it with one barbed finger.

The wind dipped, and the clouds of sand momentarily parted. Krýl looked up. "What is it?"

"It is nothing."

"It's not nothing." Krýl poked the mound again.

"It was something, but now it is nothing." The last word was snatched by the rising wind and sent tumbling off to the west.

Krýl put his hand against the mound and gave it a shove. It rocked forward and then back, shedding sand. Mezka tugged the hýthric forward. This time it came with only a modicum of protest. Apparently, it disliked her less than it had a moment ago.

Squatting beside Krýl, Mezka reached out and gave the mound a sharp rap with her knuckles. It made a hollow sound. Mezka waited and tapped it again. From out of the sand gathered about the base of the mound came first one scorpion, then another, then another. Mezka stood and took several steps back.

The wind quieted in earnest, and the blowing grit fell away. Krýl looked from the scorpions to the surrounding hardpan. Littering the space behind the shiny black mound were other heaps of sand. Some were large, some small. One had a wagon wheel protruding from it, another the leg of a hýthric.

"A caravan?" asked Krýl.

"No," breathed Mezka.

"I count five men, two wagons, half a dozen animals."

Mezka tucked the corner of her robe more tightly about her mouth and nose.

Krýl tapped the mound. "Does this have anything to do with that?"

"No."

"They can't have lost their way, not this close to the road."

"Does it matter?"

"It matters." More scorpions sifted from under the hollow mound, their backs shining in the sun. "If these weren't accidental deaths it matters a great deal."

Mezka lowered her gaze and kicked at one of the scorpions that had wandered too close to her toes.

With a grunt, Krýl reached down and picked up one of the scorpions. He held it in the palm of his hand. The arachnid waved its pincers and curled its tail. In the half-light Mezka could see that its carapace was nearly translucent, only its back and the tips of its pincers were stippled with black.

"Daughter of Agonies," said Mezka.

Krýl turned his hand. The scorpion waved its tail. "Is that its name?"

"If it stings, you will be a long time in dying."

Krýl raised his hand to eye level. The scorpion continued to present its sting. The wind gusted, throwing sand against the mound. Mezka could hear the hollow clatter from within.

"Pretty little thing."

"It is a female. She is not quite grown."

Slowly, Krýl lowered his hand. The scorpion gave one last wave of her tail, then scuttled sideways into a crack in the hardpan. The man in the living armor stood, looked down at the mound.

"What is this thing?"

"It is a shell."

"What sort of a shell?"

"A shell."

Beside her, the hýthric shifted and grumbled. Mezka reached out and touched its neck, patting it.

"It's an awfully big shell."

Mezka could hardly hear him over the wind. Another gust rose to gale force and Krýl disappeared behind a veil of sand. When he reappeared he was closer. Mezka jumped and took a step back.

Krýl tilted his head to one side. "You alright?"

Mezka looked down at her feet. "We should not stray from the road."

Krýl regarded her, the yellow membranes over his eyes flat and expressionless. After a moment he gestured in the direction from which they had come.

Mezka pointed in the opposite direction. "It is that way."

"It's a road," said Krýl, "it goes from one place to another. If we go in that direction," he pointed again, "we're bound to run into the godsdamned thing."

"Not this road."

Tugging at the hýthric's reins, Mezka faced into the wind and shuffled towards the spot where the road should have been. If she was lucky, it would still be there.

Mezka shook her head, loosing a cascade of sand. She dug her fingernails into her scalp, bent over, and shook out even more grit. When she stood up straight, her head swam. Sitting herself gingerly on her blanket, Mezka drew a deep breath and let it out slowly. Her head began to clear. Across from where she sat, Krýl chuckled.

"Go ahead and laugh," said Mezka, wrinkling her nose.

"Go ahead, man who does not have any hair on his head to get sand in."

Krýl tugged at the thin, russet beard that clung to his chin. "I'm not entirely without sympathy."

"It is not the same."

Krýl smiled and raised his hand, palm out. Mezka scowled, lifted her fist, and swiped it sideways. Hard.

"What?"

"What you just did, that is not polite."

"This?" Krýl held up his palm again.

"It says to me that you are finished with me, that you no longer want to be in my company."

Krýl regarded his hand, nodded his head, and gave an approving frown. "That pretty much sums it up."

Narrowing her eyes, Mezka pressed her lips into a thin line.

Krýl smiled. "It was a joke."

Mezka turned up her nose and looked at the sky. Overhead there were stars, a glittering bow of them spread from one horizon to the other. They shone like castoff gems, a distant scattering of riches far, far out of reach. Drawing a deep breath, Mezka puffed a white cloud across the arch of stars.

"The caprices of this place are…different."

Mezka dropped her gaze. "Caprices?"

"Moods."

"Ah." Mezka glanced back at the stars, then down at Krýl. "The wind, you mean."

"Among other things."

"The wind blows when it wishes to blow."

"And yet there are no crystals mixed in with the sand, no blood red little razors that strip leaf from branch, bark from tree, flesh from bone."

"We are too far south," said Mezka.

"The crystals don't seem to care." Krýl picked up a handful of sand and let it slide through his fingers. "The storms move further each year, taking whole kingdoms."

"Perhaps it is our wind that keeps them away."

Krýl shrugged. "Perhaps."

Mezka sat for a time watching her breath, frosty and cold. Around her the air was still, only the occasional puff of wind moving runnels of sand along the surface of the hardpan. She wished she had fuel with which to make a fire. It was an imprudent thing to do out on the hardpan, but she wanted a fire nonetheless.

"Are you cold?"

Mezka glanced at Krýl's silhouette. "No." She tugged at the blanket around her shoulders. It was thick, and warm, and every day smelled less like the deviant that had previously occupied it.

"Hungry?"

Mezka wiggled her hand back and forth.

"Could be—"

"Tell me something."

Krýl sat up straighter. "What would you like to know?"

"This bounty of yours, this man you are chasing—why is he so important?"

"He's not."

"And you chase him anyway?"

"I do."

"Because it is your job?"

"Among other things."

"What things."

The man in the living armor shrugged again.

"You do not know?"

"I do not wish to say."

"You should say." Mezka sat up straighter as well. "I have showed you where he will go; I have kept you from getting lost in the desert. You should say why you continue to chase this man."

"Because it's the polite thing to do?"

Mezka pursed her lips. "No, because I am doing this thing with you."

"Alright." Krýl paused while he chewed the idea over. "I caught a glimpse of him."

"When?"

"Before I hired you. I almost had him, but he slipped by me and out into the desert."

"You saw him, and this makes you want to chase him?"

"When I took the contract I did it for the money. Now that I've seen the man, the situation has become a bit more… personal."

"You chase him for yourself."

Krýl nodded.

"You know him?"

"No, I don't know him, but I knew someone very much like him."

"A friend?"

"Of a sort."

"An enemy?"

"No. We were both the guests of a woman who collected—shall we say—unique individuals. She kept us as pets. It didn't end well."

"You were a slave?"

"I didn't think so at the time. Not at first." Krýl shrugged. "The man I'm after looks very much like one my fellow guests. I'd like to ask him a thing or two."

Mezka turned her head and looked at the place where the stars met the straight line of the horizon. From where she sat, it appeared as though the sky itself had come down to earth.

"Tell me something," said Krýl.

Mezka did not take her eyes from the stars. "What do you want to know?"

"What makes you so certain my bounty has gone to Dhulkant?"

"Because," said Mezka, "there is no other place for him to go."

"There are settlements. You said so yourself."

"They are nothing; just a well with a few huts made of mud and bricks."

"That sounds like a good place to hide."

"Strangers cannot hide in these places," said Mezka. She shifted her weight, tucked her legs under her. "In the settlements every face is known. A stranger would stand out. Besides, they would not give him water."

"I see," said Krýl. He fidgeted, took a pinch of dust and let it run through his fingers. "He could have doubled back through the cactus."

"No," said Mezka. "The only place a stranger could go is to Dhulkant. He would not be safe anywhere else. If he passed through one place then came back again, they would put him in a cell. They would suspect he is a bandit and that he is looking at their settlement so that he can tell others about it."

"Hospitable people, these Kommhadi."

"They are not," said Mezka.

"I know, I was just—"

"Making a joke."

When he spoke again Mezka could hear the smile in Krýl's voice. "And so were you."

Mezka's lips turned up at the corners. She lifted a hand

and covered her face with a corner of her robe.

"So it's to Dhulkant our friend has gone," said Krýl.

"It is."

"And where do you suppose he will go once he gets there?"

"There are places in the lower city that do not ask questions. Unless he knows someone in the upper city he will not be permitted to enter. The rich are jealous of their place and the upper city has many guards."

"That's nothing new. Anyway, I'd be surprised if he knows anyone in Dhulkant."

"We will look in the lower city then."

From where it sat a few paces away, the hýthric grunted and swished its tail. It sounded annoyed.

"I think we've upset your friend."

"He wants to sleep. We should do the same."

"You go ahead," said Krýl. "I'll take the first watch."

"I get to wake up in the middle of the night and look out at nothing until the sun comes up? What a kindness you show me."

"Is that another joke?"

"No."

The man in the living armor chuckled.

Mezka lay down with her head pillowed in the crook of her arm, the deviant's blanket pulled up to her chin. Not far off, Krýl sat looking out across the empty plain, a black shape against the backdrop of stars.

The hut was not large, perhaps a single room with a dilapidated goat shed attached to one side. The goats it might have housed, however, were nowhere in evidence. The only living thing Mezka could see was the woman and her two children. They clung to her robes, dirty little hands wound in the frayed fabric. Beyond the children, the woman, and the hut, the sand moved in distant waves.

"What are we doing?"

Mezka looked up at Krýl. "We are letting them see us."

"We've been standing here for ages."

"They are trying to decide if we are real or not."

Krýl snorted. "Of course we're real."

"They do not know that."

"So we're going to stand here with the sand piling up around our ankles while they decide?"

"Yes."

Mezka looked back towards the woman and the two children. They had not moved.

"I need to ask them about my bounty."

"If your bounty came this way they may have seen him or they may not have seen him. If they do not think we are real they will not tell us either way."

"So go up to them and let them poke you in the arm."

"That is not how things are done."

Krýl waggled his hand back and forth. "Not how things are done…"

The woman and the two children turned away and started back towards their hut.

"Where are they going?"

Mezka lifted her feet from the sand that had piled up around her ankles and shook them one at a time. "They have decided we are real. They are going back to their home."

Krýl took a step in the direction of the hut. Mezka caught his arm. He stopped and looked down at her. "What?"

"There is no man in the house. If there was, he would have showed himself to us. Because there is no man you must stay out here."

"With the hýthric? He doesn't like me."

Mezka handed him the reins. "You will have to hold him anyway."

Krýl held the reins limply in one hand, while the hýthric shifted and grumbled.

Where the woman and her two children led, Mezka followed. The hut was further from the road than she had expected, the hardpan between it and the road broken and fissured. Before she crossed the threshold, Mezka looked back at Krýl. He stood awkwardly amidst the wind and sand, the hýthric tugging at its tether, trying to distance itself from him.

Inside, the hut was dim and hot. The ceiling was low, the walls caked in soot from the fire pit set in the middle of the floor. The dung fire was just ashes now and there was no fuel stacked against the wall. The floor had once been tiled, but the simple octagons were cracked and sunken.

The woman and the two children stood before a counter set along the far wall. The woman had her back to Mezka, while the two children stared at her from between the folds of her robe. One looked to be a little boy, the other a little girl. It was difficult to tell beneath the grime caked on their clothes and faces. Both children were missing their right arm from the elbow down. The little girl cupped the stump in her left hand, while the little boy tried to hide his behind his back. When the woman finished what she was doing and turned about, Mezka saw that she had prepared tea, or at least tea of a sort. Without dung for the fire she had simply steeped the tea leaves in water. This she presented, first setting the pot and then cups on a low table beside a glassless window. As she did, Mezka saw that the woman's right arm ended at the elbow in a knot of scar tissue.

The woman gestured towards a place at the table, then situated herself on the floor opposite. Mezka joined her, took the offered cup, and sipped. The tea was not very good. She did not complain, simply took another swallow and set the cup aside. Reaching inside her robe, Mezka took out a dried biscuit, then another. A little more digging revealed a third. She gave them to the woman.

For a time they sat in silence. Mezka sipped her tea, the woman and the two children munched their biscuits.

"A man came this way," said Mezka at last.

The woman looked up from her biscuit. Her eyes were very dark, the skin around them sunburned and wrinkled.

"He had a strange look to him."

The woman lowered the remains of the biscuit, set it on the scuffed surface of the table.

"He would have been alone, riding hard."

Raising her left hand, the woman made a fist and let it drop.

"Which way did he go?"

Slowly, the woman turned her head and stared out the window in the direction of Dhulkant.

Again reaching beneath her robe, Mezka removed another three biscuits. They were the most palatable of the food she had taken from the deviant's saddlebags and she was loathe to give them up. She gave them to the woman anyway.

Getting to her feet, Mezka touched her forehead, her lips, her chest. The two children watched her move towards the door, their eyes wide in their dirty faces. The little girl fingered the place where her arm ended abruptly at the elbow. The little boy adjusted his tunic, trying to hide his scars. Then, Mezka was outside and moving back in the direction of the man in the living armor. He stood where she had left him, holding the grumbling hýthric.

"He came this way." Mezka spoke as she passed Krýl by, moving towards the road.

Krýl peered over her shoulder at the hut, then back at Mezka. "They saw him?"

"They saw him."

"How long ago?"

"They did not say."

"Did you ask?"

"No."

Now several paces behind, Krýl moved to catch up, tugging the hýthric behind him. "Why not?"

"They would not have given an answer we could understand."

"What's that supposed to mean?"

Mezka gave the hut her own backwards glance. In the shadowed doorway she could just make out the faces of the two children. "They do not understand time as we do."

Krýl tucked his chin into his chest. "That doesn't make a damned bit of sense. All they have to do is count the days."

"More days may have passed for them than for us. Or perhaps less. It is difficult to say."

Krýl shoved the hýthric's reins into Mezka's hands. "Time does not move differently for different people. The sun goes up in the morning and down in the evening." He glanced skyward. "Right now it's in the process of doing the latter."

Mezka raised her fist and swiped it sideways. "When you are out on the hardpan sometimes time acts differently."

Tossing up his hands, Krýl turned about and stared down the road. "A road that moves and days that are longer for some than others…"

The road in question appeared, packed earth edged by stones. Mezka took it, quickstepping towards Dhulkant. She passed Krýl on the left, putting the hýthric between them.

"Why the hurry?"

Mezka did not respond.

Krýl pushed his way around the hýthric and stepped up beside her. "Those children…it looked to me like they were missing their right hands."

Mezka bit her lip, wiped a hand across her dribbling nose and wet cheeks.

"What about the mother?"

Mezka tried to wave him away. He stayed where he was, matching her pace.

"She only had one hand as well."

"All three of them?"

"Yes."

"Is it—"

"It is a matter of honor."

For a time Krýl did not speak. The sand blew, the sun beat down, the road wound its way towards Dhulkant. Mezka kept her pace though her calves had begun to burn.

"What sort of honor demands that a child should have its arm cut off?"

"For the Kommhadi, it is not such an unusual thing."

"Not an unusual thing?" Krýl could not keep the incredulity from his voice.

"There are many things their honor demands."

"Like mutilating children?"

Mezka pressed her lips tight and spoke through her teeth. "Honor is a part of their law, and their law was given to them by their god."

Krýl turned this over in his head for a moment before responding. "Just the one god?"

"Yes, just the one."

"How did they choose which one?"

"The Kommhadi say their god is the only god."

"So what about all the others?"

Mezka's brow furrowed. "I do not understand."

"If the god of the Kommhadi is the only god, why doesn't everyone else believe that as well? I've heard of hundreds of gods and everyone seems to have an opinion on which is the one true god of gods."

Mezka swiped her hand angrily to the side. "It does not matter. The Kommhadi have their honor and their god. That is enough for them."

His gaze focused on the distant hardpan, Krýl said, "Their god sounds like a bit of a cunt."

Five

"Someone left in a hurry."

Krýl toed a plate made of beaten tin, one of five that sat on a reed mat in the center of the small room. The room's single window let in an anemic bar of sunlight that was hung with motes of dust. In the center of the mat stood a bowl of what had once been someone's dinner. Now it was shrivelled and caked in grit.

From her spot by the door, the girl peered at the mat, the plates, the bowl. She then went back to examining the wall. Someone had scrawled something there, carving it into the plaster with a knife or a sharp stick.

"Anything of interest? Dire portents? A Warning?"

"Just obscenities and one claim on the honor of a woman name Naahqib."

"And what is Naahqib supposed to have done?"

"Here it is said that she lay with a hýthric and then put its cock in her mouth."

"Unlikely."

"It is still a difficult slander for a woman to live down."

"Poor Naahqib."

Mezka reached out, touched the words, then drew her

hand back. "You are probably right. I do not think that this thing is possible."

Krýl snorted. "No, I don't suppose it is."

Mezka turned from the wall with its scrawled collection of invectives. She tapped her stick twice on the hard-packed dirt floor and raised her eyes to the ceiling. Her gaze did not have to travel far. Were the ceiling but a few inches lower, every step Krýl took would gouge furrows in it with the crown of the carapace.

"I do not think this is the place."

Krýl raised a hand and touched his fingertips to the ceiling. "This place isn't what?"

"I do not think this is the place where I stayed with my master. It is very similar, but it is not the same."

"Are there many of these sorts of places on the hard-pan?"

"No," said Mezka, still staring at the ceiling, "not so many."

"What are you looking for?"

"Nests."

"Nests?"

The girl kept her eyes on the cracked and peeling plaster. "Weaver nests. It is not such a good thing if there are weavers. They like places that are warm and wet. At night they will leave their nests and find them."

"That," said Krýl, casting his own eyes towards the ceiling, "is certainly cause for concern."

Outside the wind gusted and the remains of the shutters that hung askew over the window clattered. Mezka at last took her eyes from the ceiling. "I will go and find a place for the hýthric. It is not decent to leave him outside, not when we are inside."

Krýl glanced down at the girl, then back at the low roof

of the hut. "We should find a place for all three of us. Better to make sure our only pack animal is right where we can see him."

Mezka disappeared out the door, her black robe catching the wind and fluttering out beside her. The skulls slung at her waist clattered and clacked against one another. Krýl watched her go and wondered what a weaver's nest might look like.

Stepping from the room with its abandoned feast, Krýl followed the girl into the wind. It took his own cloak and set it to fluttering and snapping. He tried to gather it up, hold it tight, but it was too tattered. Between the wind and the serrated surface of the armor it had been reduced to rags and buckles.

Taking the hýthric by its bridle, Mezka led the animal between what remained of the modest collection of mud-brick buildings. There had been eight of them, all clustered about an eight-sided structure that housed an eight-sided well. Krýl had already looked inside and discovered that the well cap was off. As Mezka disappeared around the back of one of the huts, Krýl glanced through the archway that led to the well. Inside, the light was dim and dusty. Two steps brought him to the place where the well cap had been shoved to the side. He toed the flat slab of stone just as he had toed the plate. It did not move.

From where it had secreted itself, somewhere in the back of his head, the armor urged Krýl forward. Bracing his palms against the side of the well, he squinted over the edge. Beyond the circle of light halfway down the side of the shaft there was only darkness. With a sigh, Krýl extended his left arm.

The familiar sensations of having his body robbed of nutrients pricked at him. Krýl closed his eyes. When he opened them again he saw the tail end of the feeding tendril snaking its way down into the darkness. A five count later and the tendril encountered something thick and wet. Mud.

"Damn."

Mezka could not drink mud. He could not drink mud. The only thing that could drink mud had already begun to do just that.

Slowly the symbiote began to filter the water in the well from the muck that had been dumped into it. Krýl felt the armor's urgency begin to wane. He waited while it dug deeper, pulled in more water, and spat out sediment. When the armor made to withdraw the tendril Krýl told it to stay. It resisted. When he told it to siphon up as much mud as it could, the symbiote balked. He told it again and again it refused. Finally, Krýl threatened to throw himself down the well and the armor relented.

Mezka met him as he stepped from the eight-sided structure that housed the well. When she saw that he was carrying a bulging sack at the end of the armor's feeding tendril she made a disgusted face and drew back.

"It's not what you think." Krýl hefted the distended section of carapace. It sloshed.

"Water?"

"Not exactly." Krýl nodded towards the edge of the settlement. "You find a stable?"

Mezka bobbed her hand. "It is around the back."

"How drafty is it?"

As if to emphasise his point, the wind blew a fearful gust.

"When the doors are shut it is a fine place. More room than any of the huts."

"Well then," said Krýl. "Lead on."

Mezka had not been lying. With only the two of them and their single animal, the stables were spacious. When the doors were shut the wind was kept mostly at bay. Their hýthric had already taken to the place, settling itself down in one corner, chewing on a bundle of grass the girl had found tucked into an alcove.

"Sit." Mezka indicated the spot where she had set the saddlebags and laid out the deviant's blankets.

"We can't stay."

Mezka looked pained. "Why not?"

"We've lost enough time already. The wind and the dust keep blowing us off course. If we want to make Dhulkant before the water runs out, we need to keep moving."

"This does not make sense."

Krýl stiffened. "Of course it does. If you don't want to die of thirst, we need to reach the city before the water's gone."

Mezka pointed at the distended bit of carapace. "And what is that?"

"It's mud."

"Mud has water."

"Mud is mud."

"Why did you bring it then?"

"I have an idea."

"If you have an idea then why are you pushing for us to move on? This place is out of the wind, there is water of a sort, and there is something for the hýthric to eat. I think you want your bounty and that is all."

Krýl sighed. "It's the middle of the day."

"Good. We need a rest."

"It's the middle of the day," Krýl went on, "and unless you haven't noticed this whole place has been torn down."

"Not the stables."

"All save one of the huts is in ruins."

Mezka tried on another shrug.

"Someone obviously thought this place needed to be rendered uninhabitable. They tore down the buildings, knocked the lid off the well, and filled it with dirt. That sends a pretty clear message; this place is closed for business."

"Even in the best of times," said Mezka, "places like this did not have so many people. There was little business."

"I think you're missing the point." Krýl took a step forward and seated himself on one of the blankets. The distended bulb of carapace made a wet noise. With his chin he indicated the saddlebags next to the girl. "Hand us that gourd, would you?" Mezka did so. Krýl opened the stopper and positioned the sack of mud over the empty gourd. He then told the carapace to repeat its trick, to separate the water from the sediment. After a moment's hesitation it did so, pissing a thin stream of brownish water into the gourd.

Mezka's eyes went wide and she clapped her hands together. "So, it is good for something other than killing."

Krýl narrowed his eyes and tried to keep the thin stream of water on target. "Listen, whoever decided to tear this place to bits may come back through. We don't want to be here if they do."

Mezka made a dismissive gesture. "If they do, you can cut them into pieces and then let your armor eat them."

Krýl paused for a moment, readjusted the aim of the water. "Better to avoid that sort of thing."

"Why?" said Mezka. "You killed all the deviants back in the settlement. You killed the three birds." She glanced down at the skulls tied about her waist. "Why avoid killing anyone ever?"

The last of the water dribbled away and the symbiote began to complain about the wad of earth now tucked in its feeding tendril. Krýl held the tendril away from where he and the girl were seated and allowed the armor to disgorge its burden. It did so with a plop. Mezka looked queasy.

"The price of being alive," said Krýl.

Mezka waved his words away. "You did not answer my question. You, who are so good at killing, say that it is better not to? Why?"

Krýl considered the question for a moment. "People begin to notice."

"What, that you are good at what you do?"

"There are plenty of men who are good at killing."

"I have known some of them," said Mezka. "You are not like them. In their wildest dreams they could never be as good at killing as you."

"You don't know that."

Mezka leaned closer. "I do know. I have seen you."

Slowly, Krýl placed the stopper in the water gourd. He passed it to Mezka who set it to one side.

"Why avoid it?"

"Is this a test?"

"Answer my question."

Krýl sat back, crossed his legs, and rested his palms on his knees. "It's like I said, people take notice. They notice someone like me the same way they notice the deviants. Stand out too much and someone you'd be better off not knowing will make you their business."

"And this has happened?"

"You might say that."

"Better to take a job for bounty on a single man than to lead a whole army?"

"From your lips to the gods' ears."

Outside the wind did what the wind was wont to do, howling across the hardpan, pushing sand through every crack and crevice in the stable. Krýl listened to it howl, listened to the hýthric chew, listened to Mezka hum softly to herself. She did so with her head down, her stick held in the crook of one arm. At her back were the saddlebags, beside her the water gourd. Krýl watched her for a long while, light from a chink in the door playing over her neck and the side of her face.

Their approach was from upwind, the smell of fear and a week in the saddle as thick as a ground fog. After their stench came the scuff of feet on hard-packed earth. They tried to move quickly and quietly, failing at both.

Krýl sat in the dark and listened as the five men took up their positions. Three stood to the side of the stable door, the remaining two beneath the window that gave onto the hayloft. Over the sporadic gusts of wind and the slither of moving sand Krýl listened to their hearts thud and their breath quicken. When one of the men began to count slowly under his breath, Krýl got to his feet and moved to the door. He stepped through just as the count ended.

One of the men struck his chest, bouncing off and landing on his backside in the dirt. The second gave a shout and drew back a short sword for an over-handed swing. Krýl caught the arm and broke the man's wrist. The sword clattered to the ground. The third man came at him from the side, dagger aimed at his ribs. Krýl kicked him in the knee, breaking it at a right angle. The man fell, howling.

Extending the armor's feeding spike, Krýl drove it into the swordsman's middle. He kept the spike where it was, draining away whatever the symbiote found inside, while the man gurgled and twitched.

To his left someone was shouting and cursing. Krýl glanced to the side, saw it was the fellow who had bounced off his chest, and loosed the tendril from his unoccupied wrist. He cut a neat line across the man's throat, then jammed the tendril into the wound.

With both spike and tendril hard at work, the symbiote flooded Krýl's brain with dopamine and endorphins. As it ferried nutrients from corpse to carapace, the chemical reward grew. Krýl shut his eyes and put back his head.

From inside the stable there came a crash and a scream. Krýl's eyes fluttered open. With a sigh he dropped the two corpses and shoved his way back inside.

Mezka was pressed into a corner. In front of her stood the hýthric with its hindquarters pointed towards the two men who had been situated beneath the hayloft. One of them was on his back clutching his stomach, the recipient of a kick from the dromedary. The other hovered uncertainly, knife in hand. His eyes flitted from Krýl, to Mezka, to the hýthric, and back again.

Krýl snapped his fingers. "Don't look at them, look at me. I'm the one you should be worried about."

The man tensed.

With a twitch of the wrist Krýl drove the barbed tendril through the man's chest, just to the left of his sternum. He dropped without a sound.

"How many was that?" Krýl counted on his fingers. "Right, this one makes three dead, and two knocked on their arses."

Coughing, wheezing, the recipient of the hýthric's back foot rolled to one side and began to crawl away. Krýl took a step in his direction.

"Wait!"

Krýl glanced to where Mezka stood, half obscured by the hýthric.

"Please."

Krýl lifted his foot and stomped down on the crawling man's head. Beneath his heel he felt bone give way.

Mezka turned towards the stable wall, her hand over her mouth.

"Not to worry," said Krýl, "there's another one outside."

Mezka shuddered and shook her head.

"Come now, I'm sure he'll be more than happy to answer our questions."

The last of their nocturnal visitors lay on his back blubbering, his hands hovering around the smashed remnant of his knee. There was a stain on the front of his tunic. Even in the dim light of the stars Krýl recognized the man.

"You, sir, should be ashamed of yourself."

The man rolled his eyes, tossed back his head, and gritted his teeth.

"To make travelers pay so much for water ought to be a crime."

The man continued to grimace and squirm.

Krýl stepped forward and tapped the man's foot with his own. The man screamed.

"You're a long way from that shitty little settlement, friend. A long way from the forest of cactus."

"Cacti."

Krýl looked up to see Mezka emerge from the confines of the stable. In one hand she held her stick; with the other she held her robe tight about her throat.

"A cluster of cactus are called cacti."

"Huh," said Krýl, "didn't know that." He tapped the man's foot again. "Did you know that?" The man screamed.

Mezka drew level with Krýl. She looked down at the man writhing on the ground. "It is the water seller. The one you asked about your bounty."

"So it is."

"What is he doing here?"

"It's funny you should ask," said Krýl. "I was just going to pose the same question." He refocused his attentions on the water seller. "What are you doing here, friend?"

The water seller groaned, writhed, groaned again. He began to pant.

"Not what I asked." Krýl kicked him hard in the shin. The water seller howled. "Why are you here, on the hardpan? Why'd you try to take us in the middle of the night?"

Through tears and spittle, the water seller choked out an oath, then went back to whimpering incoherently.

Leaning forward, Krýl took the man by the front of his tunic. Lifting him from the ground, Krýl held him in midair, his injured leg dangling. The water seller squirmed, tried to pull away. Krýl shook him.

"Tell me!"

"After—" the water seller began, then fell to choking and coughing.

Krýl drew his arm down until the water seller's face was only a foot from his own. "After what?"

"After you took…the deviants apart…we were told to follow you."

"Who told you?"

"The same man who hired us to watch you while you were in the settlement."

"Is that why you and your friends were skulking around the streets before the deviants started tearing things up?"

"Yes…" wheezed the water seller. Krýl shook him again. "Yes!"

"Who was this man, the one who hired you?"

"I don't know."

Another shake, this time harder. There were more tears from the water seller.

"Who was the man that hired you?"

"I don't know, I don't know…please!"

Krýl dropped the water seller. He fell to the ground with a thump and set about screaming into the dust. The wind lifted, blew runnels of sand between the ruined buildings and against the back of the stricken water seller. Krýl turned to Mezka.

"He tracked us from the settlement, past the glass thorns, all the way to the hardpan. That smacks of either dedication or desperation."

Mezka watched the water seller wriggle like an injured snake. "He's in pain."

"He would've stuck a knife in you."

Mezka's eyes wandered to the remains of the two other men, then came back to rest on Krýl. At his wrist the tendril lashed impatiently back and forth.

"Why would someone pay to have him watch us?"

"Why would someone pay to have him take a crack at us?"

The water seller was praying now, rocking back and forth, sweat running down his forehead and darkening his armpits. Krýl went to him and knelt beside his shoulder.

"Who told you to kill us?"

"The same man who told us…to follow you."

"What did he look like?"

The water seller gasped for air, then said, "He looked… he looked like a rat."

"A rat?"

"Small eyes, pointed nose, big front teeth…a rat!"

"And why does this rat want us dead?"

"Your…bounty."

"Now we're getting somewhere." Krýl tapped the water seller on the forehead with his index finger. "What is it about the man I'm chasing that has this rat of yours so upset that he would send a water seller to stab us in our beds?"

"I don't know."

Krýl reached for the water seller's shattered knee.

The water seller shoved at Krýl's hand. "I don't know, I don't know—I swear!"

Krýl slapped the knee anyway.

"I don't know!" The water seller fell back, his mouth wide, his eyes squeezed shut.

"Looks like he doesn't know." Krýl stood.

"Please," said Mezka. "No more."

"Fine."

Krýl lifted his left hand and the tendril went to work. Mezka turned away and wandered back into the stables. She emerged a moment later with the saddlebags over one shoulder and the hýthric's tether looped around her fist. As she led the animal past Krýl she said, "We are going to sleep in one of the huts. You may sleep someplace else."

While the tendril siphoned off blood and offal, Krýl watched Mezka disappear around the side of the single un-ruined hut. When she was out of sight, he gave what was left of the water seller a kick. "You shit. Now look what you've done."

THE CITY

One

The goats were scrawny things, all bandy legs and round bellies. Their tails were up, their ears flapping as they ran. Krýl watched them trot by, hooves clattering over the hardpan. Behind them came a boy with a stick. It looked very much like the one Mezka carried with its water gourd swinging from one end. On his back was a pack made from a blanket tied with a length of braided hide. From head to toe the boy was covered in reddish-yellow dust; only the dark circles around his eyes showed through the grit.

Beyond the goats and the boy moved other shapes—people and livestock, wagons and hýthric. They streamed from east to west, cutting across the open plain, not bothering with the road. Beyond the people and livestock, wagons and hýthric, drifted a great column of dust, reaching for the crimson sky in tattered bands. Overhead, more dust hung in a thick pall, darkening the day, muting the light.

"This is not good."

Krýl looked down at Mezka. "The weather? No, it's terrible."

Mezka snorted. "The people, they have brought their belongings with them." She pointed to the shapes moving through the streaming clouds of red and yellow. "This is not something people usually do."

Krýl squinted at one of the wagons. It was loaded with furniture, trunks, vases, tapestries. It had been drawn by a single hýthric. Now the animal lay sprawled on its side. The over-laden wagon shuddered in the wind, its canvass top torn to rags. Around it a group of four men and one woman scrambled, shoved, argued. Krýl waved a hand in their direction. "All these people making for the city, does it have something to with the storm?"

Woodenly, Mezka shook her hand back and forth. "The wind comes every year. In this place the people have learned to live with it. No, they are going to the city for another reason."

"Only one reason I know of that can explain so much panic and stupidity."

Mezka looked up at him and blinked. Caught in the folds of her robe, not far from her right eye, glimmered a tiny speck of red.

"Correction," said Krýl, "I know of two reasons."

In the distance the shouting rose in pitch. The wind carried a few choice phrases to Krýl. He and Mezka turned towards the wagon in time to see one of the men cuff the woman to the ground. She covered her head with her hands as more blows fell. When another man shoved the first away from the woman, the first man turned his anger on the interloper. Krýl watched as the two grappled beside the dead hýthric. "That won't end well."

Again, Mezka squinted up at him. "You could do something."

"No."

"You are stronger than that man."

"What would my getting in the middle of their fight accomplish?"

Mezka continued to squint up at him.

Krýl shook his head. "If I beat him, made a fool of him, he would just take his anger out on the woman later. If I killed him in front of the others, then all of a sudden I'm the one who looks like a bastard. Better to let someone from their own group sort this out."

"It is not right." Mezka gritted her teeth and jabbed a finger towards the sad little tableau. "You can stop this!"

"I can stop it for a moment; I can't solve their problems. Besides, we have someplace to be."

Mezka followed Krýl's gaze towards the west.

The towers of Dhulkant rose above the mounting columns of dust, their sides lit by the westering sun. Minarets and cupolas, onion domes and diaphragm arches stood stark and unsparing against the blood-red sky. The city itself was built on a tor that rose perhaps two-thousand feet above the hardpan. Around it, Krýl could make out three concentric walls, each higher than the last. The tops of the walls were crenulated, their sides divided by enfilading towers, their gates staggered. The people dotting the plain made for the nearest of these, scuttling like so many grubs for the shelter of that lofty stone shell.

Krýl put a hand on Mezka's shoulder. The girl pulled away, her eyes still on the two men and the cowering woman. Where Mezka gripped her stick her knuckles had gone white.

"You should do something. They will kill each other if you just stand here."

"They drove their hýthric into the ground hauling a load of furniture and carpets. Can't say I have much sympathy for people who would do a thing like that."

"Then keep them from doing it again!"

The wind dropped, a pocket of calm descending over the plain. Where swirling columns of dust had a moment ago reached towards the sky, there was now only stripped hardpan dotted with moving shapes. The armor balked and Krýl turned himself in a circle.

The girl went stiff. "What is it?"

Krýl looked skyward. "Shit."

The shapes that hurtled from the sky were black as pitch. They struck the two men who had been grappling and bowled them over. Men and birds landed in a heap, arms and wings flailing. The woman screamed as another shape fell on her back. Within a two count she had disappeared beneath a fluttering canopy of feathers and talons. One of the men reached for her, then set about doing his own screaming as an armored beak struck him in the back of the head.

Mezka shrank against Krýl, clutching at his arm.

Krýl looked down at the girl. "So, does this mean you've forgiven me for the water seller?"

The man that had been struck in the back of the head lost most of his scalp. Mezka shuddered and Krýl put an arm around her.

Two more of the great carrion birds descended on the wagon and its occupants. They flapped and hopped, gouging and striking at its panicked occupants. A sixth bird lit on the flank of the dead hýthric and buried its face in the animal's belly.

Even through the armor Krýl could feel Mezka shaking.

She had a hand pressed to her chest, the tip of her stick and the water gourd lashed to it trailing in the dust.

"Come." Krýl turned Mezka towards Dhulkant. She resisted. He lifted the girl from her feet and set her down facing towards the city. He gave her a push and she took a few stumbling steps in the direction of the nearest gate. Krýl followed. "There's nothing we can do for them. Not now."

Mekza rounded on him. "You could have done something before the birds came!"

"No." Krýl pointed towards the sky, to the empty space left by the lull in the wind. "They were already overhead, just waiting for the right moment. If I had gone over there I would have been in the middle of that mess when the wind dropped."

Mezka raised her eyes and her mouth fell open. Black shapes hurtled earthward from out of a great kettle that seemed to hang motionless above the plain. Krýl counted forty of the birds before turning his attention back to those already on the ground.

"Where did they all come from?" Mezka gaped. She took an unsteady step and nearly lost her balance. Krýl took her by the upper arm and began a quick step in the direction of the city.

"Ask me again when we're inside."

There were guardsmen at the gate, enough to form a complete phalanx. However, they had chosen to forego that tried-and-true formation in favor of a more haphazard position. Instead of standing with their shields locked in a unified front, they were busy stripping the personal belongings from the men and women trying to enter the city. Working in groups of two or three, the guardsmen blocked the path of anyone still carrying anything more than the clothes on their backs. With swords drawn, they demanded the refugees hand over jewelery, food, livestock, packs, purses, and the occasional set of footwear. Krýl saw the goats that had been driven by the dusty young boy off to one side, milling about in a frightened circle. The boy was nowhere in sight.

Beside the goats and against the wall of the gatehouse were half a dozen young women that had been stripped to the waist. They stood facing one another, their arms crossed over their breasts, their heads down. They were flanked by guardsmen, steely-eyed and with a jealous look about them. At the girls' feet an ever-growing pile of bags, satchels, and trunks threatened to tumble sideways.

As the crowd pushed itself closer to the gate, eyes fell on Krýl and the girl. Some lingered, some slid off. Krýl faced front and watched as one refugee after another was relieved of everything and anything worth taking, then shoved through the gate's vaulted arch. Once on the other side they stumbled aimlessly, knocked from side to side by other unfortunates, until the tide of moving bodies carried them further into the city. From there Krýl could only speculate where they might go and to whom they might turn.

"Ow!" barked Mezka. "Ow, my foot!"

A fat man pushed past her, shoving Mezka against Krýl. He caught her and eased her around behind him.

"Hold my cloak."

"What?"

"Grab a handful and don't let go."

"How am I supposed to carry my stick and the hýthric's reins if I am holding onto your cloak?"

"Give me the stick then."

Someone jostled Krýl from the right, someone else from the left. He jabbed with an elbow and made himself a little breathing room. From behind him Mezka said, "I cannot give you my stick."

"Then give me the reins."

"No, the hýthric does not like you. He will not follow you."

"Then give me the stick!"

The hýthric, perhaps jostled beyond the point of endurance, perhaps smelling the fear coming off the crowd in waves, chose that moment to kick. A man caught a two-toed foot in the stomach and was knocked to the ground. The surrounding mob began to shout, then they began to shove. Someone screamed. Over the heads of the throng, Krýl saw the guardsmen lift their eyes and peer towards the rising commotion.

"Stick or reins, choose one!"

The girl handed over the hýthric's reins. Krýl started forward, tugging the unwilling beast behind him. The girl came after, one small fist knotted in the tattered mess of his cloak. The shouting grew in volume and was joined by the sounds of blows falling and men grunting. Krýl gave it another minute before someone would unsheathe a blade and chaos would ensue.

"What are they—"

"Don't look back, don't let go."

Krýl plowed ahead, ignoring those who had turned around to gape at the quickly forming riot. Where he found an obstacle in his path he used the jagged surface of the armor to grate and scrape his way through the crowd. Behind him Mezka made frightened noises and the hýthric brayed.

Another scream rose, fell, and was joined by a high-pitched wail.

"Don't look back."

"But—"

The fat man who had stepped on Mezka's foot hove into

view, his feet firmly planted. Krýl kicked him in the back of the knee, then slapped his left ear with the flat of his hand. The fat man howled and fell over. Krýl used his back as a step and hauled Mezka and the hýthric up and over.

A gust of wind swept in from the east, driving a stinging wall of sand against the crowd. Ahead, Krýl could see the guardsmen shift nervously. The young women who had been stripped to the waist huddled closer together and the goats began to bray. Krýl watched the faces of the guardsmen, looked from one weathered veteran to another, before at last coming to rest on a young man whose beard was no more than a wisp. He angled for the boy in his ill-fitting leather and bronze.

"What are they doing?" asked Mezka. "Why are they taking the people's bags and animals?"

"Payment," said Krýl.

"For what?"

"If you can't pay or won't pay, they won't let you in." He gestured to the curving length of wall on either side of the gate. Along it huddled hundreds of people, their possessions clutched to their chests or piled up beside them.

"That is not right," said Mezka. Krýl heard a sob in her voice. "It is not right!"

"Who said it was?"

More sand was thrown against the crowd and against the walls of the city. Krýl ignored it and dug one hand into the pocket sewn into his cloak. The press of bodies tightened. He made one final effort, shoved his way forward, and stopped in front of the young guardsman.

"Yours," said Krýl, pushing the reins of the hýthric into the boy's breastplate. "Yours," said Krýl, shoving a loose collection of ingots into the boy's hand.

As cylindrical coins fell from the guardsman's fumbling

grasp to ping and clatter on the cobbles, Krýl reached to the back of the hýthric and tugged the saddlebags free. With them came the water gourds; not as many as had been tied there an hour ago, the rest having wandered away in the crowd.

Putting an arm around Mezka, Krýl tossed the saddlebags over his shoulder. He stepped around the young guardsman, who was bent over trying to scoop up the fallen ingots, and made for the shelter of the gate. He managed a dozen steps beyond the great bronze doors before another guardsman put himself in Krýl's way. Krýl ground the man's toes under his heel without breaking stride. As the guardsman yelped and fell sideways, Krýl shoved Mezka forward into the streets of Dhulkant.

Two

"There are so many…" Above the length of cloth she had tucked over her mouth and nose, Mezka's eyes were wide and bright. "Where will they go?"

Krýl grunted.

Mezka worried a tear in her robe. Sand clung to the faded black cloth making it appear even more worn and frayed. More sand was caked on Mezka's forehead and cheeks. Krýl felt his own face. The absence of the carapace had left a layer of sand on his features.

"All these people…" Mezka gestured with her head towards the lines of men and women tucked against the sides of buildings, in alleys, and perched on the tops of walls. They were filthy, dishevelled, bereft of all possessions save the most basic. Most simply huddled or stared at the ground. A select few looked on like hungry aýrs-hounds, sizing up each new passer-by. "There are more than I can count."

"I didn't even bother. Most of the countryside must be packed in here."

Mezka sniffed and made a new gesture with her hand.

"What does that mean?"

Mezka shrugged. She was getting better at it. "Mostly it means that I am sad, but I am also afraid."

They walked on for another twenty steps before Krýl said, "That's probably wise."

The light was beginning to go, fading from a sky still choked with dust. Over the city's spires, black shapes continued to circle, occasionally diving into the canyons of cut stone. In the lower city where the streets were narrow and the lamplighters had not deigned to come out, the winding avenues were filled to overflowing. Krýl had already seen a dozen fights for possession of what, a day ago, had only been another gutter. Now that same gutter was home to whoever could hold it against those who would take it from him. Women and children seemed the most notably dispossessed. Matrons hurrying along five, six, even seven children moved from place to place, alley to alley, looking for a spot to call their own. Few found one.

Mezka stumbled, cracked her toe against a loose cobble. She hissed, hopped up and down, clutched at her ankle. Krýl held out his hand. She waved him away. "It feels as if we have been walking for hours."

"We have."

Krýl looked up, past the dark bulk of looming domes and palisades, at the pointed tip of a minaret. The last of the daylight had painted it a deep arterial red.

Mezka stopped, balanced on one foot for a moment, her stick planted in the cobbles. Lifting the other foot she examined the stubbed toe. It had begun to bleed.

"We'll need to get that seen to."

Mezka glanced up at him. Before she could speak, someone jostled her from behind. Krýl caught her before she toppled over. For an instant he entertained the idea of shoving his fist clean through the man that had pushed past. After a three count he unclenched his fingers and took a deep breath.

"Come on."

"Where?" Mezka's shoulders slouched as she surveyed the crowded street, the people crammed into every possible nook and cranny. "Maybe we should just find somewhere and lie down."

Krýl readjusted the saddlebags and the water gourds slung over his shoulder. "The word has already spread about a man and a woman who made it into the city with a bag and with water. If we stop out in the open, whoever's been listening to those rumors will come looking."

Mezka sighed. "So we walk."

"So we walk."

Krýl looked back down towards the wall, then up at the towering keeps and temples on the tor above. He put his hand on the girl's back and guided her forward. "I've an idea."

The streets of Dhulkant rose in elevation just as they rose in station. As alleys gave way to avenues, so to the lower city gave way to the middle city, the middle city to the upper city.

The slums that abutted the walls were little more than empty shells occupied by vagrants, squatters, and the dispossessed. As the streets moved up and away from the walls, tenements appeared, as well as warehouses, tanneries, and stockyards. These were open to the sky, blazing cauldrons where the poorest of the poor made a living amidst heat and squalor. Beyond the warehouses and tanneries stood inns, brothels, and taverns that masqueraded as teahouses. The spirits distilled in their basements and back rooms wafted a chemical stench through the streets and up into the workmen's quarter. Here craftsmen of low caste made goods for the home, goods for the soldiery, goods for the men and women whose terraced gardens overlooked the district. Those goods flowed up to the merchants' villas, past the one hundred temples of Dhulkant, then into the upper city proper. Once in the upper city the streets widened, becoming regular in their orbit. Bounded on four sides by the wide, cobbled streets, each block was a fortress unto itself. Hanging gardens could be seen above the walls, their trellises covered in vines and many-hued flowers. Guardsmen patrolled behind the crenulations that topped the walls, the tips of their spears and helmets moving at a slow, steady pace. At street level, mosaics ran the length of the walls, a pictorial testament to those who dwelled within. Made of colored glass, shaped by the workmen in the city below, they showed lineage, deed, and faith. Beside the mosaics stood watchmen, the city guard called out in force, stationed around every bend and corner.

Krýl stood in the shadow of an overhanging trellis, the vines blocking the light from the nearest lamp, watching the watchmen. Unlike in the lower city, here the lamplighters had been forced from cover and made to ply their trade.

Mezka's breath came short, sharp, and loud. Krýl was surprised the watchmen had not already heard her and raised the alarm. Putting out an arm he pressed her further against the wall. She closed her hands around her stick and steadied her water gourd.

"We should not have come here."

"Quiet."

The watchman shifted his weight from one foot to the other. He leaned on his spear. He was not as well armed or aromored as the men that guarded the walls. Still, he had a voice and he had confederates.

"We should not have come here."

"Be quiet."

"We are not high caste; this is not a place for us."

Krýl glanced at the surrounding keeps, their high walls, the torches on their battlements. Though the sky was dark, the streets were bright, the shadows chased away by those with enough money to make them run.

From down the street there came the sound of footsteps. Krýl peered around the corner and saw another watchman approaching. His steps were unhurried, but his eyes were alert. Krýl pulled back.

The second watchman stopped beside the first and they exchanged a few words. The second watchman then moved on, rounding the corner and heading up towards the next block.

"You've got a point," said Krýl.

"About what?"

"About being here, on the street." Krýl patted his shoulder. "Grab hold."

Mezka blinked.

"Go on." Krýl turned his back to her and knelt down.

Reluctantly, Mezka stepped forward and put her arms around his neck. Krýl got to his feet, then gave a little hop to situate the girl. She let out a small sound of protest but did not let go. Krýl moved to the wall and set the barbed tips of his fingers into the narrow cracks between the stones. Lifting himself with his arms he braced the balls of his feet against the wall and began to climb.

As soon as he left the ground, Krýl felt Mezka tense. She clung to him like grim death, her breath whistling in his ear, as he pulled himself past the trellis of vines and towards the top of the wall. He glanced back once and saw a watchman shuffle past the spot where he and Mezka had hidden themselves. At the top of the wall Krýl hooked one arm between the crenulations and peered along the walkway below. When he saw no guards, Krýl pulled himself up and over.

Squatting behind the parapet, Krýl tried to unfasten Mezka from around his neck. She would not let go. As gently as he could, Krýl worked his fingers beneath her arms and levered them over his head. Mezka, her knees trembling, sank to the walkway.

"Not here."

Taking Mezka by the arm, Krýl pulled her to where the walkway gave onto a covered terrace. Once they were beneath its shadowed arches, he let her drop. Mezka, her stick still clutched in one white-knuckled fist, went to her knees and lowered her head. Krýl gave her till the count of ten.

"Up."

She shook her head.

Krýl reached out, tried to take her arm. She batted him away.

"C'mon, we can't stay here."

"We should not be here at all."

"You want to go back to the lower city, to the streets so choked with people there's barely a place to step let alone sit?"

Mezka raised her hand, made a gesture.

"What's that mean?"

"It does not matter. We should not be here."

"Is this because you're afraid of trespassing, or is this some residual guilt about your caste?"

Mezka looked at him, dark eyes wet with tears. They had cut furrows in the grime that clung to her cheeks. "If I am caught in the upper city I will be impaled. A sharpened pole will be put into my rectum, and I will be lifted over the wall.

It will take hours to die."

"All because you entered the upper city?"

Another tear fell. Mezka wiped it away leaving a muddy streak below her left eye. "I was a slave."

"To hell with that."

Krýl dragged the girl to her feet and pushed her towards the nearest door. She stumbled along, her legs barely able to hold her upright. When they reached the door she slumped against the wall beside it. Krýl tried the latch. The door was locked. Pressing the tip of his fist against the narrow space between the door and its jamb, he extended the feeding tendril. Probing, feeling his way along the far side of the door, he eventually found the latch, and lifted it. As the door swung inwards, Krýl took the girl by the arm and slid inside.

The pool was lit from below by a quartet of spheres, one set at each corner. The light was a faint blue, reflected by the tiled mosaics overhead. Mezka watched the liquid pattern flicker across the laid glass, mouth open, stick hanging from one hand. Krýl reached out and took it from her lest it fall with a clatter.

The girl raised her hands to her lips. She looked down at the pool, then back up at the gentle waves cast against the vaulted ceiling. Krýl laid her stick gently on the floor.

The grotto was not large, but it need not have been. Within its four tiled walls was enough water to choke a heard of hýthric. Trying to take it all in at a glance, Mezka wavered on her feet.

"Sit down before you fall down."

Mezka shook herself. Krýl pointed to the floor. She pursed her lips.

"Suit yourself. But if you crack your head open, I'll let the armor lap at whatever leaks out."

Mezka made a disgusted noise, but gently lowered herself to the tiled floor. From this vantage she continued to alternately watch the pool and its reflection on the ceiling.

"You still afraid of being impaled?"

Mezka trembled. "If we are caught in this place I do not think they would wait to impale me."

"And what would the owners of this keep do to me?"

"I think, perhaps, if we are discovered you would kill them first."

"I think, perhaps, you are correct."

Mezka looked sideways at Krýl. "Yes, I think you would do this thing."

"I don't see another option."

"Then I do not think I will do so much worrying."

"For the best."

Mezka raised her head.

Krýl unfastened the remains of his cloak and let it drop. He kicked it to one side, closed his eyes, and took a deep breath. He focused on the symbiote, on his own heartbeat, on the gentle slosh of the water in the pool.

At first the armor fought him, stubbornly refusing to let go. Then, by increments, it began to pull back in on itself. Krýl kept his eyes shut and his breathing steady until, all at once, the symbiote receded, disappearing into a jagged ridge along his spine.

Mezka gasped. Krýl shivered. He lowered his arms and turned around. The girl was looking at the far wall and chewing on her thumbnail. Krýl glanced down at himself. His flesh was very pale save for his hands. Against the smooth white of his forearms they looked like dusty leather. He had no doubt his face looked very much the same.

Moving to the far wall, bare skin prickling, Krýl stepped into a low tub. Beside it was a ceramic pail overhung by a spigot. After a moment's fussing he managed to open the spigot and a thin stream of water dribbled into the pail. He opened the spigot wider, filled the container, then shut it off. When he lifted the pail, he noticed Mezka watching him out of the corner of her eye. As he raised the pail over his head, she looked quickly away.

Krýl poured. Krýl shivered. Krýl felt the dirt caked on his face and head begin to loosen. He filled the pail again, and again poured it over his head. The third time he filled the pail, he set it gently on the tiles in front of him. Scooping out water in both hands he scrubbed at his face, his chest, his back, his underarms and groin. He scrubbed until the trail dust was gone, spiralling down the drain at one end of the shallow tub. When he raised himself from the tub, he noted that Mezka was again watching him. This time she did not look away.

"Where did you learn to do that?"

Krýl cocked an eyebrow. "What, you think I'm a ruffian who's spent his whole life sweating in the desert?"

"I did not say that."

Krýl stepped from the tub and made his way towards the pool. Beneath his feet the tiles were wet and slick. "I spent some time with a woman of means. She had the largest bath I've ever seen, so big you'd think it was a small sea."

As he lowered himself into the water, Mezka said, "When was this?"

Krýl thought for a moment. "Three years ago." He lowered himself further into the blessed chill of the pool.

Mezka smiled and turned her head to the side. "Your penis was very large, but when it touched the water it shrank."

Krýl, the water now up to his lips, spluttered and coughed. Mezka laughed, then clapped a hand over her mouth. Raising his own hand, Krýl flicked water at her. Mezka shied away.

"Go on," said Krýl, gesturing towards the low tub and the ceramic pail. "You'll feel like a whole new person."

Mezka lowered her eyes.

"Go on."

For a moment Mezka sat unmoving staring at the tiles. "What?"

"You must promise not to look at me."

"Why? You had no compunctions about noting the unfortunate retreat of my cock."

Mezka shook her head. "It would not be polite. I am filthy and I do not want to be seen that way."

Krýl shrugged. "If it's that important to you, then I won't look."

Mezka hesitated, then got to her feet. Krýl turned away. He moved to the middle of the pool, parting the water before him with languid strokes. He listened to the sound of the girl's robe falling away and stared at the glowing spheres at the bottom of the pool. A moment later and she was at the tub filling the pail, emptying it over her head, scrubbing, filling it again. It was a long time before she finished.

"Careful," said Krýl. "Floor's slippery."

The sound of Mezka rising from the tub and padding to the pool stopped just shy of the water's edge. Krýl looked up.

She was very thin, her hips narrow, her features slight. She stood with her arms tucked beneath her breasts, her head turned, one leg held to the side. Her hair was dark, glistening wet, plastered to her temples. A single bead of water slipped down her cheek to the sharp line of her jaw. When she drew breath, Krýl could count her ribs. When she dropped her arms and stepped into the pool he could see the bones of her hips move beneath her skin.

As the water touched her calves Mezka gave a little shiver.

Her nipples hardened and she lifted her hands to cover them. As the water touched the dark patch of hair between her thighs, Mezka shuddered and lifted her eyes to the ceiling. Krýl watched as the surface of the pool slid over the brand set high on her left thigh. In the space of another heartbeat she had sunk to her shoulders.

"You look like someone who's never taken a bath before."

With a slosh and ripple Mezka turned herself towards Krýl. "I have never seen so much water in one place before."

"What about in your former life?"

Mezka shook her head. The motion seemed almost natural. "Sometimes, with the other slaves, I was allowed to go to the baths. The tubs were very small; the water was always too warm. If I was unlucky and I was the last one in line, the water would be brown and filled with dirt. The pleasure girls were always the first to bathe. They received the best food, the best clothes, the best of everything."

"You don't sound particularly enamoured with them."

"Stupid cunts." No sooner had the words left Mezka's lips then she clapped her hands over her mouth and sank further into the pool.

Krýl chuckled. "Tell me what you really think."

Mezka shivered. "I should not have said that."

"But you did."

The shiver returned and remained. Mezka's teeth began to chatter.

"Are you still worried?"

Mezka nodded.

"Caste strictures run deep, eh?"

"They do." Mezka looked as though she might fold herself into a ball and sink to the bottom of the pool.

"Never had a caste. Don't feel the need for one now."

Mezka thought about this for a moment. "Perhaps we should not speak. Just to be safe."

"I did remember to lock up once we were inside."

Mezka gave him a knowing look. "You have done this sort of thing before."

"If I thought I could get away with it, yes," said Krýl. "As a boy I made of point of sneaking into other people's bath houses."

"Why?"

"Because, every fortnight or so, I got fed up with being dirty and poor."

Mezka lowered her face into the water then lifted it, wiping droplets from her eyes. "So, you stole into other people's houses and used their water?"

"I did. Ate their food as well."

"Were you ever caught?"

"Once."

"What happened to you?"

"I was beaten and locked in a storeroom."

"And then?"

"And then I used a broken piece of a pottery to lift the latch and escape."

"They did not find you again, these people who caught you and beat you?"

"No."

"And after that, you became a mercenary and you started hunting bounties."

"Something like that. Had a bit of growing up to do first. Lost my hair in the process." Krýl patted the smooth top of his head.

Mezka giggled.

Krýl smiled, listening to the slosh of the water against

the sides of the bath.

"These things at the bottom," said Mezka taking a step forward, pushing against the water, "what are they? How do they shine under the water?"

"The sun."

"They are not the sun. Do not say such things."

"Every ten days, maybe twenty depending on how old they are, you put them in the sun. They take in the light and give it back a bit at a time."

"You have seen them before?"

"I have."

"Where?" Mezka moved closer, eyes fixed on the glowing spheres.

"The same place I saw the bath, the large one."

"They do not get hot, these…orbs?"

"No." Krýl moved to the side, took a deep breath, and slipped beneath the water. When he came up again he was holding one of the spheres. "Here. Take it."

Hesitantly, Mezka reached out and took the sphere. Her expression brightened. "It is not hot at all."

"No. Just a ball of light."

Her eyes fixed on the glowing thing in her hand, Mezka moved closer. "From the old world?"

"One of the old worlds, at any rate."

Mezka took another step forward and let the sphere drop. As it sank it cast moving shadows across her face, her neck, her shoulders. Krýl watched as the spot of light came to rest at the bottom of the pool, picking out highlights along the girl's slender frame. Mezka took one final step and pressed herself against him.

"You—"

Her lips touched his. They were soft, and cool, and wet. Krýl put his arms around the girl and she pressed herself against him, wrapped a leg behind his. Her tongue flicked past his teeth. He could feel her small breasts against his chest.

Mezka pulled back, bit her lip.

Krýl touched the corner of his mouth with the tip of one finger. "You don't know how to nod or shrug, but you can kiss? How odd."

Mezka smiled showing straight, white teeth. She put her hands on Krýl's shoulders and again pressed her lips against his. Krýl slipped a hand around her waist, traced the contours of her back and buttocks. She kissed him harder. He touched her between her thighs and a shudder ran the length of her frame. Mezka whimpered, held his face in both of her hands. Her lips were parted, her breath hot against his cheek. Krýl lifted himself and pressed into her. Mezka gasped and melted against him.

Water sloshed against the sides of the pool, slipped over its rim, spread across the tiles. It came in rhythmic waves accompanied by low cries and little whimpers. Mezka held tight to Krýl, nails biting into his shoulders. She held tight until her voice rose and she began to writhe and buck. A moment later Krýl let himself go, gripping the girl around the waist until he was spent.

For a time they held one another, the slosh and ripple of the pool slowly dying away. Krýl felt himself grow limp and he sank down until only his head and nose were above the surface of the water.

Mezka pushed herself backwards. She floated away from him, drifting, until her back touched the side of the pool. She grasped its edge, turned her face to the wall. Krýl watched her, his heartbeat thudding in his ears. She did not look up.

Three

Holding the gourd in one hand and the ceramic pail in the other, Krýl poured. Most of the water made it into the waiting mouth of the gourd, but some of it slopped over the side and went dribbling away.

"Damn."

Krýl tried again. He did better this time, hardly losing a drop. It seemed the key was to only put a splash in the bottom of the pail and to pour it out in a thin stream.

"You look strange."

"Do I?" Krýl set the pail aside. "What makes you say that?"

From where she sat on a low couch made of wicker, Mezka waved absently in his direction. "Without that thing covering your face I can read every thought that goes through your mind."

"Can you now?" Krýl turned his head from side to side. "What am I thinking?"

"Mmm…" Mezka tugged at the towel wrapped around her shoulders. "You are concentrating very hard."

"Water is a precious thing."

Mezka stretched, yawned. "Every time I look around and see your face I wonder, who is this man? He cannot be the same one I saw in the settlement. He cannot be the same one who killed all of those deviants, or the carrion birds, or the water seller."

"That was as much the armor as it was me."

Mezka shifted position, ran a hand through her damp hair and down her cheek.

"How's your toe?"

Mezka cracked one eye, swivelled it towards her foot. "It is alright."

Once out of the pool, the toe had started to bleed again. Krýl had wrapped a strip of cloth around it which he had torn from a towel. He was surprised that the symbiote had made no overtures towards lapping up the blood. In fact, it seemed to be ignoring Mezka altogether.

"The man you are looking for," said Mezka, her eyes again closed, "the man the deviants were also looking for. How will we find him now? The city is overrun, there is something going on outside the walls, and we are hiding in someone's private bath."

"Bit of a conundrum," said Krýl. "I'll give you that."

"So, what will you do?"

"Is that question rhetorical? I'll do some asking around, same as before."

Mezka shifted position again. Beneath her the wicker creaked. "Who will you ask?"

"You tell me. You're the one who's been here before."

"We will have to go back to the lower city."

"Not the best place to be right now."

"The water we have will trade very well. With so many people inside the walls the price will be very high."

"Good point. Though I still have money. That also trades very well."

"We could sell some of the water," said Mezka. "That will get us more money. This, I think, will be easier to carry."

"Another good point." Krýl picked up the pail and started to pour.

The girl stirred, the towel she wore falling from one shoulder. Krýl saw bones moving beneath her olive skin.

"Before we do anything we should get you something to eat."

"More sleep first."

Krýl considered. "Not here."

"Why not?"

"Someone might want a bath."

"It's the middle of the night."

"It was the middle of the night. Now it's going on towards morning."

Mezka lifted her head in alarm. "How do you know? There are no windows."

Krýl tapped the side of his nose. "I know."

Hastily, Mezka got to her feet and shed her towel. Krýl watched her slim backside jounce as she tip-toed to where her robe hung. She felt the cloth, decided it was dry enough, and slipped it over her head. The washing she had given it in the tub beside the pool had dislodged half a desert's worth of sand. While it did not look new, it was a sight better than it had been. Krýl's own cloak had not fared as well. He doubted if it would last the day.

Mezka went hunting for her sandals, found them, went back to the wicker couch, and began lacing them up. "If we are going back to the lower city, we will need to do it before the sun comes up. If we are caught out in the open—"

"We'll be impaled. I recall."

"Come," said Mezka impatiently. She waved to Krýl as she picked up her stick. The water gourd swung heavily from one end.

"You're welcome," said Krýl.

Mezka waggled the stick. "It was very kind of you. Now please, let us go before someone finds us!"

Krýl turned the spigot and splashed more water into the pail. "I wonder how they go about getting water all the way up here to the upper city."

"I was told that Dhulkant is built on an aquifer," said Mezka, teetering from one foot to the other. "The water is brought to the upper city using pipes."

"Fascinating." Krýl tipped the pail towards the mouth of the gourd.

Mezka made a frustrated noise. "Why not simply hold the gourd beneath the spout? That would be much faster."

Krýl thought for a moment, then placed the gourd beneath the spigot and turned it on. A moment later it was full. "Should've thought of that myself."

"We must go," hissed Mezka, "before the sun—"

"It won't be up for another two hours." Krýl tapped the stopper into the gourd and got to his feet. "We're fine."

From where she stood, her body taut as a bowstring, Mezka watched him tie the water gourd to the saddlebags. When this was done, Krýl lifted the rig and tested its weight. It was considerable.

"Are you angry with me?" asked Mezka. She had pulled back a step, hugging her stick to her chest.

"No. Why would I be?"

Mezka bit her lip. "Because of what happened. In the pool."

"I'm not angry."

"You look angry."

"I have several things on my mind. Not the least of which is getting back over the wall carrying you, the bags, and the water." With no small amount of effort Krýl tried to keep his mind off the image of Mezka standing naked beside the side of the pool. When he finally pushed the thought away it was replaced by the memory of her beneath his fingertips and the small sounds she had made just before she lowered herself onto him.

Mezka stood very still, her frame rigid. "I am sorry," she said, "I should not have come to you like I did."

Krýl cleared his throat and strode to where his newly washed, albeit tattered, cloak hung. He lifted it, smelled it, gave it a squeeze. Yes, he would need a new one. "There's nothing to be sorry for. I wanted it just as much as you did."

"You have been kind to me. That is all. I am sorry for my impropriety. If you are offended—"

Krýl sighed. "There's nothing to be sorry about. My honor has not been besmirched. I don't feel sullied. I don't care about the Kommhadi caste system. I don't care that you were a slave. Now, if you'll stop talking bollocks, I can focus on getting us out of here."

Mezka lowered her eyes and tucked one corner of her robe over her mouth and nose. She turned towards the door.

Holding the remains of his cloak in one hand, Krýl shut his eyes and gave the symbiote a nudge. It responded by working its way out from the ridges along his spine. A moment later it had wrapped itself around his frame leaving only his hands and his face free. The expansion cost him protein, amino acids, and any feeling of respite he had earned over the hours spent in the bath.

Slipping the tattered cloak around his neck, Krýl moved to the door, the saddlebags over one shoulder. As he passed, Mezka watched his face closely. "Your eyes," she said, "your cheeks...they look hollow."

"Sounds about right." Krýl opened the door, glanced down at Mezka, then stepped outside.

Four

Something was on fire. A column of smoke rose from the lower city somewhere to the north of where Mezka stood. She peered around the bulk of a tenement, the top four of its eight stories visible above the steep gradient that led down towards the slums and the wall. Others stood on the street or on the roofs of other tenements and watched the smoke rise. No one spoke. In the distance there was the sound of shouting, a muted wave of voices that grew loud, then soft, then loud again. Beside her, the man in the living armor stood with one hand on a carved stone railing, the other clutching the saddlebags. Most of the water gourds were hidden beneath the folds of his new cloak. He had taken it from a wash line and paid the owner with half a litre from the gourds.

"How fast will that spread?"

"The fire or the riot?"

"Both."

"If the fire is close enough to a tenement building or one of the warehouses, it will spread very quickly." Mezka swallowed. Her throat felt as dry as the hardpan. She wanted a drink of water, but did not want to unstopper her gourd. Not here, not with so many others looking on.

"Is that where we need to be?"

"No." Mezka gestured down the sloping street, its gutters still occupied by a thinning crowd of refugees. There were not as many along this street as in the lower city, not this close to the merchants' district.

"Where then?"

Mezka pointed straight ahead and to the right.

Together they stepped from the shade and into the street. The sun was just above the eastern horizon, its bloated red face distorted by the waves of heat that rose from the hardpan. Before it fled wisps of dust and the black shapes of carrion birds.

Once she was in direct sunlight, Mezka felt her skin prickle and beads of sweat gather on her forehead. Already the work she had done in the bath was being rendered pointless.

Krýl moved ahead of her, stepping around people, around piles of excrement, around heaps of rubbish. Mezka held a hand to her nose, suddenly conscious of the stench rising from the street. She had not smelled it before, but the time spent in the upper city had changed that. Once free of the reek of the lower city she had become dangerously used to fresh air. Now she gagged on the odor of a thousand unwashed people and their filth.

They passed by more tenements, more spectators mutely watching the smoke rise in the distance. They passed by a woman who had been beaten and left naked in the gutter. Her legs were spread wide and there was blood on her thighs, blood in her hair. They passed by the remains of a fire. Over it had been erected a spit. Mezka could not look at the blackened remains hanging over the dead ashes.

Off in the distance the sound of a thousand, thousand voices rose to a howl. This was followed by a crack and a rumble that shook the street. Krýl spared a glance to their left, at the smoke pouring into the morning sky.

"Don't stop, just keep walking."

Mezka drifted closer, nearly touching the hem of Krýl cloak. He did not increase his pace, but moved steadily away from the smoke and the sound of turmoil.

"The city is coming to pieces, the whole of the lower quarter is overrun with refugees, and you want to find just one man?"

"He's got a…distinct complexion."

The fat man squinted at Krýl. One eye was a brown so dark it was almost black; the other was milky-white. Mezka watched it turn in its socket and felt herself go queasy.

"Oh," said the fat man, drawing out the single syllable, "he's got a distinct complexion. Why didn't you say so?

Should be no trouble to locate him. No trouble at all."

Mezka pulled her gaze from the fat man's milky-white eye and looked at Krýl. "I do not think he is being genuine. I think maybe he is making a joke at us."

The fat man glared at her. "What gave you that impression?"

Krýl picked at the edge of the table with one thumbnail. He pried up a splinter and flicked it away. The surface of the table was tiled; only the frame was made of wood, expensive and imported. Both were chipped and dirty.

The fat man snorted.

Krýl leaned forward. "You still haven't given us a price."

"I still haven't agreed to give you any information."

Krýl drummed his fingers on the table and glanced at Mezka. "I thought you said this one would sell anything for the right price."

Mezka bobbed her fist. "He told my master many things."

The fat man levelled his one good eye at Mezka. "You're a slave?"

"No." Mezka lowered her head. "My master is dead."

The fat man swivelled his gaze back to Krýl. "You should have told me this before you sat this one down beside me, a free man. I should not be seen with the likes of her. Neither should you, for that matter."

Krýl shrugged. "Doesn't bother me."

"It should."

Krýl's thumbnail dug into the wood at the edge of the table. "She tells me things, translates for me, keeps me headed the right direction."

"She was a slave." The fat man turned back to Mezka, looked her up and down. "She was a slave who now goes about in a tattered old robe with skulls hung from her belt.

What happened to your master, little slave? Did you fuck him till his brains were so addled he set you free, or did you stick a knife into him while he was asleep?"

"He died," said Mezka to the floor, "on the hardpan. He fell from his hýthric."

The fat man sat back on his cushion, the floorboards creaking under him. "I recognize you now. You belonged to al Nahaat, didn't you? He was such a robust fellow. Too quiet, too reserved, but very good at his business. Quality smugglers are hard to come by."

Mezka bobbed her fist, a tiny, disheartened gesture. Krýl took her wrist and lowered her hand to her lap. She did not resist.

"Like I said, she tells me things, keeps me headed in the right direction. Reminding her of this al Nahaat doesn't do me any good."

The fat man dredged snot from his sinus and phlegm from his throat. He rolled the mucus around in his mouth then gobbed onto the floor. Within a three count, a spindly boy in an ill-fitting tunic was down on his hands and knees mopping up the sputum with a rag. The fat man did not look at the boy. With his one good eye he scanned the crowd, the press of bodies. In the teahouse there was hardly room to sit, let alone stand. The ceiling was too low for most men, even Mezka had had to duck. Mercifully, the air was free of the stench from the street. It smelled of incense and a hundred different varieties of tea. The increasing glare of the day was held at bay by a thick door and thick walls without windows. Fresh air was drawn into the crowded little room through vents on the roof six stories overhead.

"You came here," said the fat man, raising a hand to swat at the skinny boy who scampered away, "and asked for me by name."

Krýl lifted his chin toward Mezka. "She's got a good memory."

"You let a former slave speak my name in public."

"As you say, she's a former slave. Seems to me she can say what she likes."

"She is utterly worthless." The fat man's lips pulled down at the corners. "As a slave she at least had value. Now she is nothing. Less than nothing." He touched the downturned corners of his mouth with sausage-thick fingers and stroked the tangled length of beard that hung to the middle of his paunch. "Her master is dead, and yet she lives. By refusing to kill herself she has lost her value. She is now a shunned thing. To be seen with her is to have your honor questioned."

Krýl regarded the fat man across the table. The milky white eye did not seem to bother him, not like it bothered Mezka. She could barely stand to look at the man.

"You have insulted me," said the fat man. "You have insulted me as a free man and as a merchant. You will have to go. I cannot be seen with the likes of her."

"We just got here," said Krýl. "Our tea hasn't even been served."

The fat man shoved himself back from the table and made to rise. Krýl brought the flat of his hand down on the dirty tiles with a loud crack. Several heads swivelled in their direction, then away again.

"Sit," said Krýl very slowly, very quietly, "down."

The fat man, still poised to get to his feet said, "Why should I?"

Krýl lifted his hand, uncovering a cluster of ingots. The fat man retook his seat.

"The fellow we're looking for—" began Krýl.

The fat man slid one pudgy hand across the surface of the table towards the ingots. Krýl covered them again.

"The fellow we're looking for has a rather distinct complexion."

The fat man lifted his gaze from the money and the hand covering it. "Information costs," he said.

Krýl raised his hand, dipped into his cloak, and came up with a pouch full of ingots. He dropped it into the middle of the table. "Yours if you tell me what I want to know."

"That's if I can tell you."

"I don't think you'd still be sitting here if you couldn't."

The fat man chuckled. "You've got a point."

Reaching again into his cloak, Krýl came up with something small and yellow. He placed it beside the pile of ingots. The fat man leaned in close and squinted at it.

"A crystal?"

Krýl nodded.

"I think I know the fellow you're looking for."

Krýl plucked the crystal from the tabletop, then shoved the money towards the fat man. The fat man scooped it up and made it disappear into the sash at his waist.

"You asked for me by name," said the fat man, "Mahoud al Dashék. What should I call you?"

"Krýl."

"That's a name I'll remember," said Mahoud al Dashék with a chuckle. "That's a name I'll remember very well." He lifted his hand and wiggled two of his fingers. One of the other patrons detached himself from the tightly packed crowd and bent towards the fat man. The fat man said something to him behind his hand and the fellow turned away.

Mezka, for the first time since they had entered the teahouse, noticed just how many of the men in the crowd watched them out of the corner of their eye. Krýl did not seem to mind, but the thought of so many eyes on her made Mezka's skin crawl.

•   •   •

There were thirteen of them, all young, all dirty, all dressed in brown, yellow, and orange. They wore wraps on their heads with long tails that hung to their knees. On their chins were beards trimmed to a point, around their eyes was a thick layer of kohl. At their waists hung long knives and iron-banded cudgels. In the middle of this baker's dozen walked a huddled cluster of four: two men, two women. They were naked, their bodies scraped and filthy. They walked with their hands tied behind them, ropes on their necks. The two men and the two women kept their eyes on the ground, putting one bleeding foot numbly after the other.

Pointing to the thirteen men and their captives, Mahoud al Dashék said, "Those are Ashendi. Best we wait while they pass."

Mezka bit her lip. She watched from the safety of the side street as the men in brown, and yellow, and orange passed out of sight, their captives stumbling after them.

"What about the other four?" asked Krýl.

"The other four are also Ashendi," said Mahoud al Dashék. "They are from another clan, northerners I should think. They're being taken someplace to be dismembered."

A tremor run down Mezka's back and settled in her knees. The fat man, stuffed up against her in the narrow confines of the side street, felt as much. He sneered, swivelled his one good eye towards the men that had followed them from the teahouse. They shared a smile. He then turned back to Krýl. "It is a matter of honor, maybe the culmination of a blood feud. Now that there are too many people in the city for the guards to keep in line, the Ashendi and many others are taking the opportunity to settle old scores. Creditors have begun to disappear as well, their debtors having taken it upon themselves to wipe their slates clean. The markets are closed and the vendors are nowhere in sight. Food has become scarce. Already the city's storehouses are besieged and ready to fall. Give it another few days and the lower quarter will be in flames."

Krýl grunted.

"You've seen this sort of thing before, have you?" asked Mahoud al Dashék.

"When there's an army camped outside a city's gates, certainly." Krýl raised his head and peered in the direction of the wall. It was just visible between the buildings on the opposite side of the street. "But I see nothing out there. Nothing but sand and carrion birds."

Mahoud al Dashék chuckled. "Some say there is an army just over the horizon. Some say there are two armies. Others whisper of a crystal storm, while still others speak of gods come to earth."

"Gods come to earth?"

Mahoud al Dashék gave the tightly packed street a dismissive wave. "Whether it is an army, or a storm, or a shepherd boy frightened of his own shadow, it does not matter. Panic feeds on itself. Why do you think the whole of the countryside has packed into the city?"

Mezka shifted, pushing her way between the two men. Now that the Ashendį were gone she wanted to be out of this side street and away from Mahoud al Dashék and his bravos.

"Which way?" asked Krýl from behind her. Mezka heard the rustle of the fat man's robes as he pointed. She did not have to see him to know that he had indicated the same direction the Ashendį had taken. Mezka gritted her teeth. They stepped over a heap of garbage that contained the skeleton of a dog and into the street.

"What else do you know?" asked Krýl.

"About what?"

The fat man pushed ahead of her and Mezka was forced to sidestep around an old man sprawled in the gutter. He had sores on his face, sores on his feet and ankles. He looked at her with sunken eyes that held no expression at all.

Krýl moved up beside the fat man. "There's something you're not saying. What do you know about this crystal storm, or phantom army, or what have you?"

"Do not worry yourself about it," said Mahoud al Dashék with another wave. "You have paid me to help you find one man. This I will do. No need to let a thousand other men concern you."

"And if the whole city comes crashing down around our ears in the meantime?"

"For the right price," said Mahoud al Dashék, "I can get you out of the city as well as lead you to your bounty. You can take your man and your former slave and scuttle under the walls before this place comes down around anyone's ears."

"And what about yourself?"

Mahoud al Dashék gave Krýl a crooked smile. "Do not worry yourself about me either."

Mezka wanted to slap the fat man, to wipe the smile off his face. She concentrated instead on not stepping on refugees or their leavings.

Ahead of them, the pack of Ashendį turned to the right and started up towards the warehouse district. Mezka heard someone begin to shout. The Ashendį jostled back and forth. They raised their voices, adding to the din, and shoved their captives forward.

"There is a market square up that way," said Mahoud al Dashék. "The Ashendį will mete out their justice there."

"In an open market? Why not a back room somewhere with no witnesses?"

Again Mahoud al Dashék smiled up at Krýl. "The Ashendí like an audience."

Mezka skirted a puddle of effluent, then glanced behind her. The men from the teahouse walked three paces behind, watching the crowd, hands on the knives tucked in their sashes. Ahead of her, Krýl walked beside Mahoud al Dashék, his own head on a swivel.

"The upper city," said the fat man, "has closed its gates. Since most of the soldiers will be allocated to the outer walls, the individual house troops will guard this second curtain."

"Seems short-sighted," said Krýl. "Why not send the house troops to reinforce the men on the walls. If this phantom army or whatever it is can be kept out of the city there'll be no need for a second line of defense."

"You have never been to Dhulkant before, have you?"

Krýl shook his head.

"Here there are different worlds all existing one on top of the other. As the city rises into the air so does the importance of its people. The owners of the villas are not interested in those crawling things that live in the lower city any more than you or I would be interested in the scorpions under a rock."

Krýl glanced at the fat man. "Scorpions can sting."

"And enough stings can kill a man," said Mahoud al Dashék. "This fact is not lost on me. But tell that to the upper city. That will give them a good laugh. The ones that live so high up have been separated from the people that create their fortunes for so long they no longer understand where their wealth comes from. They think it is a thing that creates itself. They think their position could not possibly change, simply because it has not changed for so long."

They passed the street the Ashendí had taken and Mezka snuck a glance in their direction. The men in brown, and yellow, and orange were trying to force their way through a knot of refugees that had set up a tent city in the market square. Mezka hoped they would be pushed back, their captives somehow set free. She doubted this would happen. A moment later and they were out of sight, the throng that pressed them from every side blocking her view. Mezka went back to watching Krýl and Mahoud al Dashék shove their way forward.

Five

"This," said Mahoud al Dashék, "is Tezrasapoulus. You may call him Tez. He will take you where you wish to go; he will show you whom you wish to see."

From where she stood just to the left of Krýl, Mezka peered around his shoulder at Tez. Tez stood straight as a lance, his thin and angular face impassive. His eyes were rimmed with kohl like the Ashendi, but his skin was light and his long beard was as red as Krýl's. The man's bald head nearly touched the stone arch under which he stood. Mezka did her best to stay out of his line of sight. Something about his stillness and his hawkish features made her uneasy in the extreme.

Krýl looked from Mahoud al Dashék to Tez, then back again.

"Tez is one of my best," said Mahoud al Dashék. "He will take you where you wish to go, he will show you whom you wish to see."

For the space of perhaps a dozen heartbeats, Krýl said nothing. Mezka waited in his shadow trying to keep her breathing steady and her toes from twitching. She wanted to run. She wanted to run more than she had ever wanted to do anything before. It took every bit of willpower she could muster to keep herself from bolting.

Behind Tez there stood another five men. The light of the lamp held by Mahoud al Dashék only touched them peripherally, keeping the five mostly in shadow. None of them spoke; none of them moved.

"The man I'm looking for," said Krýl, "he's close?"

"Oh yes," said Mahoud al Dashék, "very close."

"How close is very close?"

"Tez will take you." Mahoud al Dashék gave Krýl a thick-lipped smile.

"I'm not giving you the rest of the money until I have my man."

The smile stayed where it was, stretching Mahoud al Dashék's face out of true. "Of course, of course. When you have your man you can pay Tez. Tez will take his cut and I will receive the rest."

Krýl leaned in towards the fat man. "How beneficent."

"I am a generous fellow." Mahoud al Dashék spread his hands. "Now, if you will excuse me, I have business elsewhere. Besides, the undercity belongs to Tez. It is his… domain."

Mahoud al Dashék turned on his heel and started back up the way they had come. It was a good one hundred paces to the mouth of the tunnel, then another fifty to the grate in the warehouse district they had used to enter the undercity. It had been Krýl who had moved the heavy iron lattice out of the way. Mahoud al Dashék and his men had done little save light a few lanterns and grumble. Now they put their back to Krýl and Mezka, moving off into the dark, taking their lights with them. As soon as they had gone, Tez struck a light of his own.

Mezka coughed, put a hand to her mouth. Krýl looked down at her.

"Dust," she croaked.

Krýl refocused on Tez, Mezka on the passageway. The arched stones hung low, while a generation's worth of dust coated the floor. There were footprints in the dust, marring the tiny dunes that stretched up and down the tunnel.

With a jerk of his head, Tez indicated that Mezka and Krýl should follow. He moved off without a word, each step making the shadows cast by his light slither along the walls. The other men fell into step with Tez, one to either side, three behind. They wore the same shapeless black robe as the tall man, their hoods up, their faces obscured. In the shifting light it was impossible to tell where each man ended, and his shadow began.

The tunnel led straight ahead for perhaps twenty paces before it began to curve to the left. With each step Mezka could feel the floor tilt, heading downward at an ever-increasing gradient. After another two hundred paces the tunnel branched to the right and then to the left. Another one hundred paces and they turned left, then right, then left. Mezka tried to keep track of the twists and turns they had made, but she gave up after the tenth or eleventh. Around her was nothing but shadow and stone, men moving without speaking, a smell like a tomb. The urge to flee grew stronger.

"How much further?"

In the thick and dusty silence Krýl's voice seemed loud and out of place. Tez stopped and turned. He tilted his head in the direction they had been going.

"How much further?" said Krýl again.

Tez stood stock still with his lantern flickering in one hand. Mezka watched the tall man for a moment, then looked to Krýl. Krýl smiled and shook his head.

"You've been leading us in a circle."

Tez did not speak, just stood and stared.

"We're maybe ten paces from the first branch you led us

down."

The other men shifted, spreading themselves to either side. Mezka gripped Krýl's arm. He kept his eyes on the tall man with the lantern.

"Did that git al Dashék pay you to lead us around in a circle, or are you working on your own initiative?" When the tall man still did not respond, Krýl sighed and said, "How about we stop this pretending and just get on with it?"

Tez lifted one long-fingered hand from beneath the folds of his robe and twitched it in their direction. Krýl dropped the saddlebags and what remained of their water.

They moved on him from three directions—right, left, and center. Krýl stepped to the side, sweeping Mezka towards the wall. She cried out as she struck the ancient stones. Krýl kicked the man on the right in the groin, felled the man on the left with a blow to the head, then caught the man in front by the throat and lifted him off his feet. The others shied away and Tez's lantern swung wildly as he staggered backwards.

"Why even bother leading us around?" asked Krýl, still holding the man by the throat. Mezka could hear gagging noises coming from under his hood, could see him struggle and kick. "Why not just knife us the moment the fat man waddled off?"

Tez steadied his lantern and glared at Krýl. His angular face was drawn and pinched, underlit by the capering flame.

"Sand-worm got your tongue?"

Tez kept his peace.

"Alright," said Krýl, dropping the man he still held to his knees. He locked the barbed claws of his right hand around the top of the man's head, twisted, and began to squeeze. The man screamed, gurgled, howled until his cries were interrupted by a wet crunch. Mezka turned her face to the wall as the crown of the man's head went to pieces. After a moment Krýl pulled his hand free, shaking off loose bits of skull and gray matter. He turned to Tez. "That didn't have to happen."

The remaining four men turned and fled. A second later, Tez dropped his lantern and bolted after them.

Pushing the nearly headless body to one side, Krýl thrust out his left hand and loosed the feeding tendril. Whipping his arm around, he slashed at the retreating Tez. The tall man fell with a shout, the first sound Mezka had heard him make. He continued to make inarticulate cries of pain as he rolled over onto his back and lifted his leg in the air. In the faint light of the toppled lantern, Mezka saw Tez's foot hanging to one side, the ankle half cut through.

"You know," said Krýl, taking a few unhurried steps towards the whimpering Tez, "I'm done. Finished. I've chased this bounty of mine from one desert to the next and been harried since the start. I'm done with being jerked this way and that, done with being fucked around. What I want now are some straight answers." He knelt before the prone figure. "Think you can give me some?"

Tez said nothing. Krýl poked him in the foot. Tez threw back his head and howled.

"Do not!"

The sound of Mezka's voice chased Tez's scream down the curving length of the tunnel and away into the dark. She listened to it go, then said again, "Do not."

Krýl looked at her with one eyebrow cocked. "Really? This again?"

"You tortured the water seller when he came for us at the way station. I did not stop you then. I should have. What you did was not correct."

"Not correct?"

Tez reached for his ankle, clasped it in both hands. His lips were squeezed shut, his eyes wide.

"You should not do such things," said Mezka, her cheeks hot, her eyes stinging. "You should not hurt people for answers."

"Alright," said Krýl, still kneeling before Tez. "How would you like me to go about gathering information from this man?"

"Why do you need information from him at all?"

Krýl smiled, lowered his head, gave it a shake. "She asks why…"

"Yes," said Mezka more forcefully, "why?"

"Because," said Krýl, looking up again, "the need for information is the whole reason we're here."

"There is an entire city on top of us!" said Mezka, her voice rising. "An entire city that is tearing itself to pieces! The guards steal from the refugees, the refugees steal from one another, the upper city leaves them all to die! All this is happening, and you are down here hurting even more people!"

Krýl cocked his forefinger at her. "About that…" He reached over and took a corner of Tez's robe. The tall man let go of his bleeding ankle and battened his long fingers around the cloth. Krýl tugged harder.

"What are you doing?" shouted Mezka. "Stop it!"

Krýl wrenched and pulled. Tez gritted his teeth and tried his best to hold on. He lost the contest. With a ripping and popping of seams, Krýl pulled the tall man's robe from around his shoulders. Mezka staggered back against the wall.

From the middle of his chest to just above his groin, a slit ran the length of Tez's torso. At first glance it appeared much like a hairless vulva, but as Mezka watched, it split and peeled itself apart with a liquid sucking sound. Inside were teeth, hundreds of them. They rippled, moving like a field of grain in a breeze. As the slit in the tall man's chest opened further, a pair of tentacles emerged, slick and red, hooked at the ends. Each went a different direction, sliding around Tez's torso, leaving behind a trail of mucus. Mezka put her hand to her mouth and tried to press herself through the wall of the tunnel.

"Could smell him," said Krýl, "all hunger and rot. He's a deviant. At least of a sort. I've never come across someone like him before, but a predator knows its own kind."

From deep in his chest, Tez let out a long, gurgling hiss. Krýl flicked Tez's heel. The hiss was cut short by a yelp of pain. Without taking his eyes from the deviant, Krýl said, "That begs the question, why are there deviants running amuck in a city governed by the Kommhadi? Last I heard the Kommhadi didn't particularly care for people like you."

Tez sneered and the two tentacles levelled themselves at Krýl. Even in the sputtering light of the lantern Mezka could see them pulsing, the long vein running down the center of each throbbing with Tez's every heartbeat.

"Put those away," said Krýl, "and answer my question."

Slowly, the deviant pulled the barbed tentacles back into the mouth set vertically in his chest.

"Better," said Krýl. "Now tell me why you're here, why Mahoud al Dashék tried to have us killed, where my quarry is, and what the hell is going on outside the walls of this city!"

Unclenching his teeth, Tez opened the mouth set in his face and leaned forward. Mezka caught a glimpse of another pair of tentacles wriggling about where the deviant's tongue should have been.

"Gods damn it," said Krýl. He sighed, rolled his eyes. "Just drag your carcass in the direction of the man I'm looking for and I'll consider letting you keep your remaining foot."

"No," said Mezka, peeling herself from the wall of the tunnel.

"I beg your pardon?" This time Krýl's expression was far less amused.

"If something is not done about his foot he will bleed to death."

Krýl looked down at the growing puddle in the sand. His feeding tendril had snaked its way across the tunnel floor and was busy sucking up what the sand had not already claimed. "You've got a point."

Scurrying over to where the saddlebags lay, Mezka dug about until she came up with a length of rope. This she tied into a sliding knot before offering it to Krýl.

"No," said Krýl, rocking back on his heels. "If you're so concerned about him, you can apply the tourniquet."

Mezka let her gaze slide off of Krýl and onto the deviant. Tez watched her with unblinking eyes, his face still twisted in pain.

The lantern flickered, dimmed, went out. Mezka opened her mouth to scream, but before any sound could escape the tunnel filled with a pale blue light. Shading her eyes with one hand she squinted at it. The light dimmed. Mezka blinked, trying to banish the after-image along with her surprise.

The light came from a cluster of stalks protruding from the back of Krýl's armor. The end of each glowed like one of the spheres in the pool now so very far above them. As Mezka watched, the stalks grew, twined about one another, and pointed themselves at Tez.

"Go on," said Krýl.

Slowly, Mezka bent and lowered the length of rope towards Tez's injured leg. The deviant did not move. She brought it closer.

"Have a go at her," said Krýl, lifting the feeding tendril from the puddle of blood, "and I'll pop out both your eyes."

Tez glared, but held still as Mezka slipped the loop over his foot. She cinched it tight just above the knee. Tez winced.

"Well, that's done," said Krýl, getting to his feet. He clapped his hands and rubbed the palms together. "If you want to live through the next few minutes, Tez, I suggest you take me where I want to go."

Six

Mezka stared out at the black expanse of water, her mouth open, her stick dangling from one hand. Krýl tried his best not to burst out laughing at the tableau. If the bath in the upper city had been a shock, this was something else entirely. It was doubtful Mezka had ever seen so much water in her life. For that matter neither had Krýl—not fresh water, at any rate.

The underground lake stretched a distance of perhaps a quarter mile at the waist and a mile to either side. A causeway had been built across the narrows, running from the tunnel mouth where they stood to the further shore. At its center was a construct of metal and ceramic, blinking diodes, and thrumming machinery. Beneath the rumble of the ancient device Krýl could hear the sound of rushing water. From the lake's surface grew a forest of stone columns that had been carved into neat, orderly rows. Set in sconces along every fifth column were spheres that gave off a steady white light. Reflected by the lake, they created the illusion of a mirror world just below the surface. Down there everything appeared silent and serene. But touch the water and that mirror world would shatter.

Krýl let out a low whistle. The reflection on the surface may have been ephemeral, but below it was wealth, tangible and immense. With this much water the elite of Dhulkant held the power of not just hegemony but life and death.

Mezka continued to gape, for the moment Tez and the Mahoud al Dashék forgotten. Krýl chuckled and tapped her on the chin. "You'd better close that thing before something crawls inside."

The girl snapped her mouth shut with a sharp click of her teeth.

Krýl turned to Tez. "And you'd better keep doing what you've been doing."

The deviant, one hand braced against the wall of the tunnel, glowered.

"Go on, boy. Fetch."

Tez hobbled forward, his wounded leg dragging behind him, leaving a smear of blood on the tunnel floor. Krýl wondered if the leg had gone numb or if the deviant felt every faltering step. After a moment's consideration Krýl realized he did not much care. He followed the deviant for a few paces before something caught his eye and ground him to a halt. Reaching out, he dug his fingers into Tez's shoulder. "What the hell is that?"

Tez glanced at Krýl, then over the side of the causeway. He snorted.

"I asked you a question."

Tez made a chopping motion with his hand.

Krýl lowered the glowing fibrils that hovered over his left shoulder and aimed them at the water. In the pale blue light he could see two men in guard's uniforms floating face up. Their throats were open, their heads nearly cut from their bodies. Whoever had done the knife-work had either been grossly overeager or had been trying to make a statement.

Behind him, Krýl heard Mezka make an exasperated sound.

Krýl prodded Tez in the back. "Whose handiwork is this?"

Tez glared at him, his face all planes and angles in the dim light.

"Was it you?"

Tez looked away.

"Fuck's sake," said Krýl, thrusting Tez forward. "I don't have time for this. Just go."

The deviant went.

After two dozen paces, Krýl felt a tug on his cloak. Without breaking stride, he glanced over his shoulder. "What?"

From behind her hand Mezka whispered, "This is not a place we should be."

Krýl gave his head a single shake. "This is exactly the place we should be."

"There is something wrong here."

"You think I don't know that?"

Krýl took a few more steps after the shuffling Tez and nearly collided with the deviant. He gave the man another shove in the back and sent him hopping ahead. Opening the vents along his throat and the sides of his torso, Krýl let the symbiote taste the air. It came back with nothing but the smell of the lake, the stone, the blood still seeping from Tez's ankle. Shaking loose the feeding tendril, Krýl dipped it into the lake. The water came back pure and cold.

"The armor doesn't smell anything."

"There is something."

"Was that something the fact that al Dashék set us up and Tez here tried to murder us?"

"That is not what I mean."

"Is it the dead guardsmen we just sauntered past?"

"That is not it either."

"If you think I don't know this is a trap then you're wrong. Of course it's a trap. The thing is, I don't care."

"We should go."

"No," said Krýl, "we should not."

Tez stopped again. Krýl pulled the tendril out of the lake, the armor hardly protesting after glutting itself on more water than even it knew what to do with.

"What is it now?"

Tez pointed.

At the center of the causeway, beside the ancient bank of machinery, a figure got to its feet. It was shaped like a man, though even from a distance Krýl could see its proportions were off. The figure was too long in the arms, too short in the torso. After pulling itself erect, the figure lingered in a patch of shadow between two of the great columns, unmoving.

"Is that him?"

Tez nodded.

"What's he doing?"

Tez turned to look at Krýl, his eyes narrowed.

"I can see that he's just standing there. Why?"

Tez continued to glare.

"Tell him to—" Krýl paused, remembering the pair of tentacles that had slithered from between the deviant's lips. "Never mind."

Beside him, Mezka tried to dart fervent glances in every direction at once. Her breathing was rapid, her pulse visible along the side of her throat. The machine at the center of the causeway thrummed and ripples ran out across the surface of the lake.

"You," said Krýl, jabbing a finger at the figure on the causeway, "walk towards me. Do it slowly."

The figure did not move. Krýl repeated his command. Still the man remained where he was.

"Damn it…" Krýl pushed Tez forward. The deviant rolled his lips back from long and pointed teeth. Krýl pushed him again. "Move. If you stop again and I'll cut your belly open and dump you in the lake."

Tez spread his arms for balance and limped forward.

"Why is the man not moving?" Mezka's words held a note of panic.

Krýl frowned. "I don't know." He gave Tez yet another shove. "And this cunt won't stop stalling."

"You almost cut off his foot."

"And yet, thanks to you and your tender ministrations, he seems to be doing just fine."

Mezka looked back at the trail of blood that led towards the mouth of the tunnel. What she saw blocking the opening made her cry out. Krýl pivoted on his heel.

The four men that had accompanied Tez stood shoulder to shoulder at the end of the causeway. Their robes were swept up and back, tied between their legs. Their hoods were down. With their loins girded and heads bare, Krýl could see they bore more than a passing resemblance to Tez. Their bald heads, long beards, and pale skin could have marked them as brothers. All, that is, save one. In place of a beard this man had long sideburns and a cleft running from his forehead to his chin. As Krýl watched, the cleft opened, pushing the man's eyes to the sides, exposing needle-like teeth and a lolling red tongue.

Mezka screamed, this time in earnest. The sound echoed from the columns, the ceiling, the water. It bounded and rebounded, coming back at them from a hundred different angles. When it died away, the sound of laughter took its place. Snapping his head back around Krýl saw Tez standing erect and grinning.

"Oh, to hell with you Tez." Krýl drew back his fist, the surface of the armor forming into the jagged semblance of a blade.

Tez saw as much and hurled himself from the causeway. Skittering to its edge, Krýl made a grab for him. All he managed was a glimpse of the deviant's robe as it disappeared into a plume of dark water.

"You whoreson!" Plunging his left arm towards the vanished deviant, Krýl slashed the water with the feeding tendril. "When I catch you, I'm going to take you apart piece by quivering piece! You hear me? You fucking hear me, Tez?" Krýl continued to hack at the water. The surface of the lake roiled.

"Enough!"

The word boomed through the cavern. Raising his head, Krýl glanced left, right, and finally back over his shoulder.

The figure that had stood alone before the ancient bulk of the machine stepped from the shadows with a rattle of chains. In the soft glow of the spheres its face seemed to glimmer and shift. Behind it, a slab of darkness detached itself and joined the figure in the light.

Mezka drew breath for another scream, but could only manage a whimper.

The second figure stood head and shoulders over the man on the causeway, a hulking mass of bone, muscle, and scales. The creature's head was set low on its shoulders, its face covered by armored plates, tusks depending from either side of its jaw. More armored plates ran along its shoulders, down its arms, across its chest. Instead of clothes or a robe, it wore strips of leather wound around its torso and groin, down its legs, and over its feet. A leather wrapped hilt protruded over one shoulder, whether from an axe or sword Krýl could not tell. The creature moved with the sinuous grace of a predator, stalking up behind the smaller man and placing a hand on his shoulder. The man sagged under its weight.

Retracting the tendril, Krýl got slowly to his feet. He glanced at the four deviants blocking the tunnel, then back at the massive shape. In the back of his mind the armor hissed a warning.

"And you are?"

There was a pause, then the oversized thing said, "One who would speak with you."

Krýl tossed his arms to either side. "And what is that supposed to mean?"

Another pause, then, "You killed my men. Butchered them."

"I've killed a lot of men."

"I would speak with the man who dismantled the soldiers I sent looking for this man." The hand on the smaller figure's shoulder squeezed. The figure sagged further.

Krýl snorted. "So you chained him here, on the causeway, as what…bait?"

"Yes."

"Fair enough. How long have you had him?"

"Five days."

"Five days…" Krýl lowered his head and pinched the bridge of his nose. "I've been knocking about this city for a day, a night, and a day, and you've had him for the better part of a week."

"That is correct."

Krýl looked up at the vaulted ceiling, its graceful arches hidden in shadow. "Fuck me."

"You killed my men," said the scaled monstrosity. "Why?"

Krýl lowered his head. "Because they got in my way."

There was another pause, long and pregnant.

"Good servants are difficult to come by. I do not appreciate what you've done."

"And what about Mahoud al Dashék?" said Krýl. "Is he one of your servants?"

"Mahoud al Dashék works for the highest bidder. At present, that happens to be me."

"And them?" Krýl cocked his thumb at the four deviants loitering at the end of the causeway. Behind him, he heard Mezka whimper.

"They've been on loan to al Dashék, but they belong to me." The creature raised its head and its nostrils flared. "They should not have run from you in the tunnels. They know better."

"They don't look like they're going anywhere now."

The creature lifted its tusked chin towards the four deviants. "If you live you may consider your earlier failure forgiven. Now go on, earn your keep."

Krýl heard a rush of feet from the end of the causeway and the armor hissed another warning. He glanced to the side in time to see the four deviants begin an ungainly charge in his direction. Krýl unslung his cloak, rolled his shoulders, and waited for the symbiote to cover his head and face. It obliged, forming crown, comb, and faceplate, covering his eyes with polarized membranes that brought the darkened cavern into brilliant focus.

The deviants howled as they came on, wordless sounds like the click and chatter of ghouls. Despite the carapace, Krýl's skin prickled.

The first of the deviants onto the causeway spread his

arms as he ran revealing a horizontal slash in his abdomen. Krýl was not surprised to see that slash open exposing teeth and tentacles. The second did likewise, baring six smaller mouths set along his ribs. The third bent forward as his back split vertically. The fourth left his face wide open, tongue lolling against his chest.

Mezka shrank down along the causeway and grasped at Krýl's ankle.

"Stay still."

Mezka withdrew her hand.

"Our large friend, is he still there?"

Mezka glanced at the tusked figure, nodded.

"Sound off if he moves."

Krýl watched the four deviants jog towards him through alternating patches of light and shadow. Krýl watched the four deviants began to flag, their initial burst of speed now spent. Krýl watched the four deviants and wondered why everything had to be such a godsdamned struggle.

When the deviants were perhaps six paces from where he stood, Krýl strode forward and swung low. The creature in the van, the mouth in his abdomen open wide and tentacles flapping around his hips, caught the razor edge of the tendril in his left knee. As his lower leg went spiralling off into the darkness, he continued to thrust forward, collapsing to the stones as his balance failed. Krýl drew back his leg and kicked the skittering, tumbling body from the causeway.

A heartbeat later, the deviant with six smaller mouths racked along his torso made a lung for him. Krýl stepped forward and rammed the blade on his wrist into the side of thing's neck. A freshet of blood drenched his arm up to the elbow. He wrenched the blade free just as the deviant with the split face came down on him like a sack of grain. Krýl planted his heels and let the armor take the brunt of the impact. In the next instant, the deviant battened the two halves of his face around Krýl's head and began to chew. Teeth raked the armor while the lashing tongue attempted to get at his eyes. From behind the safety of his faceplate, Krýl watched as the deviant's teeth broke and the contents of its mouth were worn away by the jagged surface of the armor. Blood streamed down Krýl's chin, neck, and chest. The armor lapped it up before it could reach his waist.

Taking the deviant's head in both hands, Krýl worked his fingers around the split sides of his face. He then dug in and pulled. The creature screamed, writhed, kicked. Krýl felt as much as heard the deviant's face split and tear away. When the deviant went limp, he let the body drop.

"Behind you!"

Mezka's shout did more to divide Krýl's attention than warn him. Darting a glance back towards the hulking figure by the ancient machine, he nearly missed the hurtling lunge of the last deviant.

The mouth that fell towards him was bigger than any of the others, even the slit along Tez's chest. Inside that toothy expanse Krýl could see row upon row of teeth waving and beckoning, a pair of barbed tentacles reaching for him. He drove his fist into the mouth that ran along the deviant's back and out the deviant's chest.

"Not helpful." Krýl turned towards Mezka. The girl's eyes went from saucers to pin-pricks. "The sentiment is appreciated, but I know what I'm doing. You're supposed to be watching the big one."

Mezka shuddered, wrapped her arms around herself, and turned towards the figure at the other end of the causeway. Krýl yanked his fist free, bringing with it a strand of gut. As the body of the deviant collapsed to the stones, he shook the length of intestine free and turned back towards the two figures.

"Are you going to make me fight you for that little bastard?" Krýl angled himself towards the center of the causeway and jabbed a bloody finger at the shorter of the pair. "I've come a long way for him, and I'll be damned if I let you or anyone else—"

"Hubris."

"What?" Krýl stopped short.

"Do you know the word?"

Krýl lowered his hand, the blood coating it already beginning to disappear into the armor. "Of course I know the word."

"I would imagine you do. You live it."

"The hell is that supposed to mean?"

The massive figure stepped forward, pushing the smaller man aside. "You have chased this man for weeks. To get to him you butchered my men."

"I butchered more than your men."

For a moment the creature considered what Krýl had said. "You kill so easily."

"It's what I do."

Again there was a moment's consideration. "Hubris."

"So you say."

"You assume that because you take life with such efficiency that you are justified in doing so. You assume this gives you a right to whatever else you want, this man included."

The chained figure did not move, just stood in its puddle of light, arms at its sides.

Krýl clenched and unclenched his fists. "You're wrong."

"Am I? Perhaps you would like to explain?" The creature drew the last word out, rolling it towards Krýl across the causeway.

"I caught up with him weeks ago. Got a good look at him

just before he managed to slip by me."

"And what did you see?"

"I saw a man that was unique, a man that reminded me of someone."

"A friend?"

"No."

"An enemy?"

"We were prisoners, captives together."

"You were slaves?" The tusks and the chin attached to them lifted.

"I didn't realize it at first."

"You and this other earned your freedom?"

"We took it."

"And now that you have seen this man," the tusks pointed towards the chained figure, "you wish to do what?"

"There are questions I need to ask him."

The scaled monstrosity huffed air like an agitated hýthric. "So much bloodshed for a few simple questions. I wonder, how do you justify all this killing?"

"I don't."

As the echoes of their words died away, Krýl heard the tone of the ancient machine begin to rise. It continued to grow louder and louder until, with a thud and a grinding of gears, it began to disgorge water from ports set along its sides.

"Ah, there it is. Right on schedule."

Krýl took a step back. "There what is?"

The creature lifted one massive hand and swept it towards the machine.

"What, that thing?"

"It is a pump," boomed the creature over the liquid roar. "Have you ever seen such a marvel?"

Krýl listened to the water gush and the machine grind.

It thundered gallon after gallon into the lake before suddenly falling silent with another metallic thud.

The creature pointed to the ceiling of the cavern. "The pump is older than the city. It is older than the Kommhadi. It was here long before either. The machine draws water from deep within the earth and deposits it here." He indicated the lake. "Without it, life could not exist on the hardpan."

"How do you know?"

"I read."

"You read?"

"I make a point of it."

"Then what do you need my bounty for? You seem to have all the answers."

Beside him Mezka coughed. Krýl glanced down at the girl, then back up.

"Your bounty?" The creature snorted. "You have no idea of his true value."

"And what is that?"

"Death."

In that single syllable Krýl heard the harsh weight of finality.

"Then why drag him down here, chain him up as bait?"

"It is as I said. I wished to know the man who could carve his way through a company of my best soldiers. Such a man might have been of use to me. Now that I have met him, I do not care for him. I am working towards something grand and little men like you are nothing more than a hindrance."

Mezka coughed harder, tugged at Krýl's leg. He glanced down at her again.

"The way is open." Mezka made a small gesture back down the causeway, back towards the open mouth of the tunnel. "We can go. We can run."

Krýl ignored her. "Something grand? You sound like

someone else I once knew. She had similar ideas. I brought them crashing down in blood and fire."

The noise the creature made could have been a laugh, though Krýl was not sure. The sound was more akin to the grinding of a millstone than actual mirth.

"Tell you what," said Krýl, retracting the glowing fibrils from over his left shoulder. "You can have your grand designs. I'll just take that fellow there and be on my way."

"No."

"Come again?"

"We're finished here."

Reaching up and over its own shoulder, the creature drew from the scabbard at its back the largest sword Krýl had ever seen. It had no tip, no cross guards or quillons, only a leather wrapped hilt and a single wickedly serrated edge. Stepping around the chained man, the creature moved out onto the causeway. "My name," it said, "is Arkus. Know this before I kill you."

Krýl shook loose the barbed tendril at his left wrist. It lashed the air in front of him, stood on end like a viper ready to strike. "Never heard of you."

Arkus answered with a bellow and a thunderous charge.

Seven

Mezka staggered backwards, her feet tangled beneath her, and she toppled. She struck the causeway with her hip, the shock of the impact rolling up her spine to the base of her skull. From behind her came the sound of blows, heavy and hard, the clatter of metal on stone. These were followed by a shout of surprise. Krýl hit the causeway almost on top of her, knocking Mezka flat.

A shadow blotted out the light from the spheres overhead. Mezka looked up to see the scaled monstrosity that called itself Arkus reaching towards Krýl. Grasping him by the ankle, Arkus heaved him into the air. Arms windmilling, Krýl came down a dozen yards away with another crash and grunt.

Leaving Krýl where he lay, Arkus strode to where his sword had been knocked from his grasp. Scooping up the wicked length of steel, he lifted his right arm and examined it in a pool of light. Mezka saw the cut Krýl's tendril had made in the scaled flesh. It was superficial at best. Arkus shook his bloodied wrist, took his sword in two hands, and advanced past her.

Krýl tottered for a moment, braced himself against the causeway, and pushed himself upright.

Mezka heard Arkus's blade cut the air with a sound like a thousand angry silverwasps. Krýl leapt the horizontal slash, tucking his legs under him as the sword passed inches from his toes. He came down in a crouch and lashed out with the tendril. It struck the deviant's hip and slid to one side. Arkus used the momentum of his swing to bring his weapon up and over his head. He aimed it down at Krýl eliciting another silverwasp drone. Krýl sidestepped, planted a foot on the back of the blade, and launched himself at the deviant.

Poised between two of the glowing spheres, Mezka caught the image of Krýl in mid-flight. His right arm was cocked behind his head, ragged blade protruding from his wrist. His left arm was thrust forward, barbed tendril cutting the air. One leg was bent at the knee, the other trailing extended backwards, his back bowed. Set in the implacable mask of his faceplate, the membranes that covered Krýl's eyes gave of sparks of white gold.

Arkus hit him in the stomach.

Krýl struck one of the slender stone columns with a

crunch. As the sphere ensconced in the column shattered under the impact, Mezka scrambled to her feet. She heard Krýl splash into the lake as she sprinted towards the far end of the causeway. She managed a few staggering yards before her foot came down sideways in a black puddle of blood. Mezka landed on a body split down the back by a grotesque parody of a mouth. Her shoulder dropped into the open maw, needle-like teeth tearing at her robe and the flesh beneath.

Pushing with her free hand, feet kicking at the gore spattered causeway, Mezka pulled herself free. She knelt, hunched forward, gripping her torn shoulder. Beneath her fingers she felt her own blood soaking into her already sodden robe.

Krýl burst from the water to Mezka's left, showering her with icy droplets. She raised a hand in front of her eyes and turned her face away.

Clutching at the stones, water cascading from his head and shoulders, Krýl pulled himself over the edge of the causeway. Arkus turned on the ball of his foot, brought his sword up, and swung it down like a headsman's axe. With a cry and shove, Krýl threw himself forward. The blade struck sparks from the stones.

"Go!"

Mezka glanced wildly about, finally catching Krýl's eye. He pointed towards the yawning tunnel mouth.

"Damn it Mezka, go!"

Arkus kicked Krýl in the side lifting him off the causeway. He landed beside her, a marionette with its strings cut. Mezka fell backwards, nearly landing on her torn shoulder.

"Go!" Krýl jerked his head in the direction of the tunnel. His faceplate was cracked, split down the middle. "Please."

Mezka ran.

With a bellow, Arkus swung again. Krýl ducked and

scrambled out of the way. Arkus recovered his swing and brought the hilt of his sword up under Krýl's chin. Krýl was thrown a dozen feet along the causeway landing ahead of Mezka and again she skittered to a halt. Krýl managed to drag himself to his knees just as Arkus fell on top of him.

Stones broke and buckled as the deviant hit the causeway. Splinters of rock flew past Mezka, scything away bits of her robe, cutting her arms, her legs, her side. The impact jarred her off her feet and down she went, rolling to the edge of the causeway, her legs swinging out into empty space. Digging her fingers into a seam between the cobbles she just managed to keep herself from plunging into the lake below.

Dropping his sword, Arkus raised one battering ram of a fist and slammed it down into Krýl's chest. Krýl's body lurched. Arkus drew back his fist and hit him a second time, knocking his head back. He repeated the process once, twice, three times. With each successive blow, Krýl's armored skull was driven first against the stones, then through them. Mezka clawed her way back onto the causeway as Krýl's upper body disappeared into a rising cloud of stone dust.

Drawing back his fist for another blow, Arkus suddenly jerked, thrashed, grabbed at his neck. Mezka saw a sand-colored flash of tendril pull itself free of the deviant's flesh along with a gobbet of meat. Arkus made a grab for it and was rewarded with a cut palm.

As the tendril continued to jab and harass, Krýl set about extricating himself from beneath the deviant. Once he was free, he staggered sideways, righted himself, and cupped his forehead in his free hand. Along his chest and faceplate Mezka could see great fissures in the armor like the cracks along the causeway. From these cracks oozed a dark, viscous fluid. More ichor spilled from between his fingers staining his hand and forearm. Krýl managed to shake his head clear an instant before he was yanked off his feet and sent hurtling through the air.

Mezka scuttled backwards as Krýl sailed by, leashed to Arkus by the feeding tendril. With the offending length of symbiote wrapped around his knuckles, Arkus knocked Krýl against first one column then another. Krýl grunted, swore, cried out as he was bent backwards, his shoulders nearly wrenched from their sockets.

Mezka put her hands over her head and pressed herself flat against the cobbles.

In mid-flight, his body perpendicular to the causeway, Krýl hacked away the tendril. With his wrist spitting ichor, he tumbled along the stones to fetch up in a heap. Still knotted about Arkus's fist, the tendril continued to lash and writhe.

Wiping at the blood seeping from a dozen wounds along his neck and face, Arkus bent to retrieve his sword. He lifted it in one handed and laid it across his shoulder. A few unhurried steps brought him to where Krýl lay sprawled, one arm tucked under him. More of the dark fluid leaked from the places where Krýl's armor had fractured. It pooled on the causeway, a black puddle that smelled of moist earth and decay. Arkus sniffed the air and grunted.

"Vermin."

One of the spheres Krýl had been hurled against flickered, then fell with a plop into the lake. Shadows washed over Arkus, over Krýl, over the shattered causeway.

"If you were worthy of more than contempt, I would consider killing you an honor. As things now stand…" Arkus shrugged, "I consider it hardly worth my while."

Arkus brought his sword down on Krýl's back.

The sound of metal against carapace, metal against meat, metal against bone filled the cavern. Mezka squeezed her eyes shut, covered her ears with her hands, and screamed. When her breath failed her, she drew in another and screamed again. She continued to scream until she realized the ancient machine in the center of the causeway had returned to grinding its gears and gushing water into the lake.

Slowly Mezka opened her eyes and lowered her hands. Heavy, numb, they dropped into her lap. She stared down at them, the fingers white and curled. She tried to lift them and could not. The machine continued to grind and gush, grind and gush. At last it slowed then stopped. In its place was the sound of heavy breathing.

Mezka looked up.

A few yards from where she knelt, Tez crouched with his robe clinging wetly to his waist and hips. His mouth was open, his lips pulled back from his teeth. Those teeth seemed as long as daggers. The tentacles that slithered from the slit in his chest flicked and twitched in her direction, prehensile and priapic.

Mezka began to tremble. Numbly she watched as Tez slunk towards her, propping himself up on his hands and his undamaged leg. He made chittering noises as he drew closer, rhythmic clicks that came from deep in his throat. Like dousing rods, the pair of barbed tentacles protruding from his chest led the way.

Mezka tried to shut her eyes. They would not close.

Tez scuttled forward in a rush, placed his hands on either side of Mezka's thighs. Her legs uncoiling from beneath her, Mezka slid backwards. Tez followed, hovering just inches above her. Mezka lay flat as the deviant's face drew level with her own.

Tentacles probed at the front of her robe, picking at the threadbare cloth. Mezka jerked and shuddered as they caught at the seams and her robe was torn away. She folded her arms over her breasts as the slit in the deviant's chest opened wide. Rows of teeth unfurled, a slick of drool spilling onto her bare stomach. Tez grinned, saliva tricking down his chin, dripping onto Mezka's cheek. She turned her face away.

Along the curve of her left breast Mezka felt something hard and wet. She hugged herself as another tentacle slid down her belly and past her navel. When it wandered inside the remains of her robe Mezka darted out a hand and slapped it aside.

Tez drew back, raised himself on his knees, and roared.

Mezka dropped a hand to the skulls at her waist. Taking one by the crown, she shoved it into the yawning maw in the deviant's chest.

There was a crunch of bone, a crack of teeth. Tez's howl turned into a bellow of pain. The deviant lurched sideways clutching his middle. Mezka scrambled backwards, fumbling at the second skull. She freed it just as Tez threw himself towards her.

The skull's beak took the deviant in the face, opening his cheek, laying bare the teeth below. Tez staggered back. Mezka fell after him. She drove the beak into his mouth as together they tumbled across the causeway.

Fury writ large across his face, Tez made a grab at her. Mezka slapped his hand away and brought the beak down on the deviant's neck. Blood splashed across her stomach, her breasts, her throat. She raised the skull again and drove it into the mouth that still worked to dislodge the first skull. Just as Arkus had done with his fist, Mezka brought the skull down again and again, alternating between face, and neck, and chest. Long gouges appeared in the deviant's flesh, some superficial some deep enough to expose bone. Mezka continued to hammer and cut until Tez stopped thrashing and lay in a bloodied, broken heap. Then she was crawling backwards, the skull toppling from her grasp. It made a hollow sound as it struck the causeway.

Tez twitched once, twice, and lay still.

The numbness returned, her blood running like lead in her veins. Mezka tried to stand and fell back into place. She gave up trying to run and simply knelt amidst broken stones and congealing puddles of cruor. She knelt and listened to the steady sound of approaching footsteps. They stopped at the place where Krýl lay. There was the sound of something heavy being shoved over the side of the causeway and into the lake. When Mezka raised her head Arkus was standing over her.

For a time the deviant loomed and looked, his eyes lost beneath the armored ridge along his brow. Then he knelt, folding himself onto the causeway. Even so, he was twice Mezka's height.

"Carrion birds."

Mezka blinked up at the deviant. Arkus pointed at the skulls, one still embedded in Tez's chest, the other discarded. Mezka glanced down at the skulls, then back up at Arkus.

"Where did you get them?"

Mezka pressed her lips together.

Arkus grunted. "It does not matter."

Mezka clenched her jaw, ground her teeth.

"You are small, but you have a sharp sting. You remind me of a little scorpion."

Mezka forced herself to keep her gaze steady and her breathing slow. On her bare chest and belly she felt Tez's blood beginning to harden. As it dried it tugged at the skin, drawing it tight.

Arkus chuckled. Slowly he extended one large, scaled hand. Around it was wound the severed length of Krýl's feeding tendril. It had gone limp. "Come," he said.

Mezka shook her head.

"You wish to stay here?"

Again, Mezka shook her head.

"You killed my lieutenant," said Arkus. "This is no small thing. You are entitled to take his place. Come with me and I will tell my other lieutenants what you have done. You will be held in high regard. Tezrasapoulus was much feared."

At last Mezka found her voice, though her words came out as cracked and broken as the causeway. "I do not want this thing."

"This thing is yours whether you want it or not. Here," Arkus reached to his belt and withdrew a knife. It was nearly as long as Mezka's arm. Arkus held it out to her hilt first. "Take it."

"I do not want that either."

Arkus thrust the hilt of the knife into her hand.

"His head," said Arkus.

"What about his head?"

"Remove it."

Mezka dropped the blade with a clatter. Before the echoes had died away, Arkus had picked up the knife and forced it back into her hand.

"Remove his head. Do it, or I will remove yours."

Mezka shrank back.

"You took one of my lieutenants from me. Either take his place or I will take my revenge."

For a long time Mezka stared at the knife in her hand. Then, as though watching someone else getting to their knees and making their way to the carcass of Tez, she did just that. She watched as that someone began to saw at the deviant's throat. She watched as the blade worked its way through cartilage, flesh, and between vertebrae. She watched as the head came free of its moorings and fell heavily to the cobbles.

"Good," said Arkus.

Mezka dropped the knife again, its blade sticky and wet. There was more blood on her hands, her wrists, halfway up her forearms. Mezka looked up at Arkus, Tez's bald head resting between her thighs. It stared up at her, slack jawed, tentacles trailing from between its lips.

Arkus's head bobbed slowly up and down. "You belong to me now."

"No," said Mezka, "my master is dead."

There was a pause. In it Mezka could hear the drip, drip of water in the distance. Around her the light of the remaining spheres was muted by the dust in the air.

Arkus grunted. "Who, the dead man in the lake?"

"He was not my master."

"So you are free," said Arkus. He retrieved his knife, cleaned it, slipped it back in its sheath. "I too am free."

Arkus moved closer and held out his hand.

Mezka took it.

Eight

She tried to keep the tears from her eyes, but they came anyway. The street in front of her blurred, swam back into focus. She saw moving shapes, a tide of running figures pouring down from the upper city. Their footfalls shook the earth. More tears welled up and went rolling down her cheeks. Balancing Tezrasapoulus's head in the crook of one arm she sniffed and dried her cheeks with the corner of her robe. Beside her, Arkus stood with his hands propped on the hilt of his great sword, slate-colored cloak covering him from his head to his ankles. Only his tusks and great scaly hands were visible.

In the distance there was a crash and rumble.

Arkus raised his head, drew in a deep breath. "The winds have changed."

Mezka sniffled, wiped at a runnel of snot with the back of her hand. The urge to break down and sob was almost overwhelming.

"Look, little scorpion."

Clutching the torn front of her robe, Mezka rubbed her eyes, blinked her vision clear.

"Do you see it?"

Mezka clutched at the front of her robe, clutched at Tez's head. On their makeshift tether, the skulls she had retrieved from the causeway clattered and knocked against her hip. "See what, the people?"

"Not them," said Arkus. He pointed past the spires of Dhulkant, out over the hardpan.

Mezka felt her chest tighten. "What—?"

"Have you never seen one before?" Arkus barked out a laugh. "It is a storm, little scorpion. A crystalline storm!"

Mezka's head swam. Putting out a hand, she clutched at Arkus's cloak. The deviant did not seem to notice.

Along the western horizon the sky had turned a shade of red so deep it was nearly black. Wisps of glittering carmine spiralled up from the approaching storm wall, grasping at the burnished copper sky. There they churned, fell away, then reformed and rose anew. The silhouettes of carrion birds fled southward before the storm, ignoring the plain around Dhulkant with its litter of human detritus. Within the city walls the people fled aimlessly, running, trampling, shouting. They tore down the broad avenues, packed into the narrow side streets, jammed themselves into already overcrowded buildings. Above the noise of panic and her own breathing, Mezka could hear the roiling mass of crystal. It thundered, shrieked, chimed like a wave of broken glass hurled by the hand of an angry god.

"Glorious."

Mezka choked back another sob.

Arkus glanced from the storm to the river of humanity surging around him as though he were a pillar of basalt embedded in the earth. "The storm will wash this city clean. It will scour the Kommhadi from the Earth. It will efface their murals, their spires, their statues. Their flesh will be taken from their bones, their bones worn away to dust. Only gouged and pitted stone will remain."

Mezka shuddered, nearly dropping what remained of Tez.

Arkus raised a hand, swept it over the crowd. "Do not mourn for the Kommhadi. They are nothing. They are not unique. There have been a thousand civilizations like theirs, just as decadent, just as craven. The storm will take them as it has taken all the others."

Somewhere up ahead there was a cry, a scream, a hundred voices lifted in lament. The motion of the crowd became erratic, shifting and faltering. The wave of humanity broke against an obstacle Mezka could not quite see. More screams filled the air as men and women were dragged down and trampled. Arkus chuckled.

"Do not mourn for them, little scorpion."

Beside the place where Mezka and Arkus stood with their backs to the wall of a sprawling warehouse, there came a metallic clang and clatter. Two figures emerged from the tunnel she had entered with Krýl what seemed like a lifetime ago. One was a deviant she had never seen before, a reptilian. The other was the rest of Tez. What remained of him hung limp in the deviant's arms, blood dribbling onto the pavement.

"Over there," said Arkus, gesturing to the other side of

the street. A hole had been knocked in the far wall. The reptilian ducked through followed by Tez, his heels dragging. More deviants emerged from the hole in the wall, went into the tunnel, then came back out again. They carried with them pieces of machinery and bulging water skins. Eventually one of the deviants emerged with a chain coiled in one fist. Behind him came the man Krýl had sought. Arkus raised his hand. The deviant with the chain stopped.

"Do you see that?" said Arkus. He nodded to the west.

Mezka looked from one to the other, Arkus to Krýl's quarry. Spurs of yellow crystal protruded from his cheeks, the bridge of his nose, the line of his jaw. The man stared blankly ahead, his eyes a pale and liquid gold.

"You will take me to its origin," said Arkus to the crystalline man. "You will take me into the Burning West, to the place of living crystal. You will show me the way through the storms."

The crystalline man said nothing, his eyes fixed on the approaching storm wall.

"Go." Arkus shoved the crystalline man towards the hole in the warehouse wall. "We have an hour to get ourselves out of the city. Maybe less." He glanced at Mezka. "We do not want to be inside the walls when the storm hits."

Mezka's brow furrowed, and she said in a hoarse whisper, "The tunnels are not safe?"

Arkus laughed. "They are, but after the storm has passed, we will have to wade through a sea of shards. No, we have the means to protect ourselves against the storms. Better to be outside the walls."

Several more deviants extracted themselves from the tunnel and slipped into the hole in the warehouse wall. When the last of them had gone, Arkus put his hand on Mezka's back. "Now you, little scorpion."

Mezka bit the inside of her cheek, shifted Tez's head from one arm to the other, and swallowed the lump in her throat. She glanced past Arkus at the open grate and the darkened tunnel beyond. A weight settled in her chest, heavy as a millstone. She put her back to them both and slipped through the hole in the warehouse wall. Arkus followed, blotting out the light.

The crystals sang as they fell, a discordant choir that grasped, and clawed, and cut. Over the city of Dhulkant the light fell, the blood red sun supplanted by the darker red of the storm. The people ceased to run, to shout, to claw at one another. They looked up and saw great spiraling arms of crystal reach out to them, beckon to them. Where the crystal touched flesh, flesh fell away. Where the crystal touched bone, bone crumbled. The storm did not stop with the Kommhadi, but moved on to their murals and mosaics, spires and statues. It consumed these as well, leaving in its wake naught but gouged and pitted stone.

EPILOGUE

Jórn lifted his foot. Jórn wavered. Jórn put his foot down anyway. Something under his heel crunched, something other than red crystal. Lifting his foot, Jórn toed the heap of minute shards. White showed through the crimson. Reaching down, he plucked the object from the heap. It was bone, a partial forehead and orbital socket. He turned it in his hand. The surface had been chiselled, grooved by a thousand tiny cuts.

"Not much left."

Jórn grunted and tossed the bit of skull aside. To his right, Nash sniffed, wiped his nose with his wrist, then made a frustrated noise. Jórn looked down at the rat-faced little man.

"Fucking hell…"

Nash pawed at the snot he had smeared across the white ceramic plating that covered his forearm. He only managed to smear it further.

Jórn shook his head. "You look like a tit."

Nash quit pushing the mucus around and eyed the big man. "Oh really, I look like a tit? You're dressed the same as me."

"Not what I meant."

"Then what?"

"Nothing. Forget it."

Nash went searching for a cloth in the pouch slung from his belt. Jórn looked from Nash to his own self. There were armored plates on his arms, armored plates on his legs, more on his chest and abdomen. There was even armor over his groin and backside. The helmet he had not deigned to wear was strapped to his hip. It matched the rest of the ceramic plating in every way except the bare semblance of a human face that marked its front. The pack he had strapped to his back, however, was an incongruity. It was made of leather with iron buckles. Against the pure white of the armor the pack seemed like a crude thing, a barbarous thing.

"You believe this shit?"

Jórn sighed. "Believe what, Nash?"

"Fucking look around, will you?"

Jórn looked around. As far as he could see there were red crystals glittering in the sun. They were heaped in the streets, in the collapsed shells of buildings, tucked into every nook and cranny. The stonework, what remained of it, was barely recognizable as having been part of a city. He supposed that another storm of comparable size would reduce it to nothing but a large chunk of rock sticking up out of the plain.

"How the hell are we supposed to find our man in the middle of all this crystal?"

"She didn't say how, she just said to do it."

"Well, if our man was outside when the storm hit he's been reduced to whole lot of not-a-lot. If that's the case we're wasting our time and we should just pack up our shit and go. Leave this hell to whoever wants it."

"And do you know for certain he was outside?"

Nash spread his arms wide. "How should I know? I wasn't even here when the storm hit. Were you?"

Jórn pursed his lips and looked away.

"No, of course not! This is like…like looking for a crystal in a pile of crystals."

"Poetic."

"Fuck you, Jórn."

"She told us to find him, so we need to find him."

"She's off her nut."

Jórn put a finger to his lips.

"What?"

Jórn tugged the blonde beard on his chin and stared at the rat-faced little man. He tried to impress as much meaning into that stare as possible.

"Fine!" Nash tossed his hands in the air. "Where do we start?"

"We start underground."

"Because that went so well for us the last time we went poking through a heap of ruins."

"If the man she wants us to find survived the storm, he would have done so by going underground."

"I suppose you're going to tell me you've already found a way down into the sewers, aren't you?"

"Not me." Jórn jabbed a thumb in the direction of another pair of figures clad in brilliant white ceramic. Between them huddled a smaller figure covered in a filthy brown robe.

"Him?"

"Him."

Jórn put his index finger and thumb in the corners of his mouth and whistled. When the two figures in white looked in his direction, he waved. They waved back.

"Then what the hell are we doing way over here? Let's go already."

Jórn grunted and pushed past Nash.

"What's your name?"

The man stammered something in a language Jórn could not understand. As he prattled spittle flew from his lips and tears ran down his cheeks.

"Slow down, slow down." Jórn patted the air. "Do you speak Faér or Duraal? What about Ashkant or Mheltoú?"

The man stammered some more. Jórn looked at Nash.

"All I speak is Duraal and Pashk, you know that."

Jórn scratched at his cheek. "Well, he's obviously got something to say."

Nash shrugged. "Guess if I'd just seen my whole city cut to ribbons, I'd be a blithering idiot too. There's no point in trying to get answers out of him. Just get him to lead us to the hole he crawled out of."

Jórn tried a few phrases in Faér and Ashkant before switching back to Duraal. None of his words seemed to have an effect. The man in his dirty cloak and dirty face continued to stammer, and spit, and cry. Jórn glanced at the other two men in their white ceramic suits.

"I think he's Kommhadi," said the first.

"Neither of us speak that gutter shit," said the second.

"Does anyone we brought?"

The two wagged their heads like chastened aýrs-hounds. "Glist would probably understand him."

"Glist isn't here."

Nash spat to one side. "You'd think we would've picked up an interpreter before inserting ourselves into Kommhadi territory."

"We were in a hurry."

"You mean she was in a hurry."

"Same thing."

Jórn got to his feet, dragging the stammering, weeping man up with him. He jabbed a finger into the man's chest, then mimed hiding under a rock. The man lifted his fist and shook it sideways.

"Does that mean No?"

"Probably."

Nash put his hands on his hips and squinted up at the sun. It shone down from a clear, hot sky. There were no clouds, no hint of a breeze.

Jórn jammed his finger into the blubbering man's chest again. "You tell us where you hid yourself. You tell us right now or we'll roll you down one of these streets and into a pile of crystals."

His words may not have made much sense to the man, but his tone got through. The man pointed off to the south, around the curve of one of the formerly broad avenues.

"Good," said Jórn. He pushed the man forward. "Show me."

The man looked down at his already bloodied feet, then back at Jórn.

"Fine. I'll clear a path; you show me the way." He made appropriate gestures to illustrate his point. The man seemed to get the hint.

Jórn counted two city blocks over and one up before the man stopped and gestured to the ground. An open sewer grate yawned in the middle of the street. Around its rim were bloodied handprints and a trail that led toward the high city.

"More than one of you came out, eh? Where'd your friend go?"

The man stared wide-eyed at the open sewer. Jórn stepped

forward and peered inside as well. Sunlight reached to the bottom of the pipe illuminating a small mound of crystals—whatever had leaked down when the men had climbed out.

"Well," said Nash, "if our man here had a friend that came topside with him, perhaps there's more that made it into the underground."

Jórn grunted. "I'd be surprised if there weren't."

Stepping forward, Jórn seated himself on the edge of the round hole. Beneath his armored flanks, tiny bits of crystal crackled as they were ground into the cobbles. He propped his hands on the opposite rim and slowly lowered himself into the hole. Inside the tunnel it was dark, and dusty, and the air was stale. Jórn stepped from the narrow circle of light and waited for Nash to join him. When the smaller man was standing by his side, Jórn started forward. The small diodes on his shoulders and left wrist fluttered to life as the circle of sunlight faded behind him.

"I don't think I'll ever get used to that."

"The lights?" Jórn lifted his glowing wrist and twisted it back and forth.

"The lights, the armor, the flashing things that blow holes in people…"

"You sound like an old woman."

"I'm not talking about loud music or drunks tear-assing around in chariots chucking wine bottles at people. I'm talking about these things: the armor, the lights, and whatnot. They're old. Very, very old. By all rights they should have been swallowed up by the Earth or crumbled to dust by now. Nothing this ancient should work as well as it does."

"Yet here we are."

"Fuck's sake. Does anything affect or impress you anymore? Anything at all?"

Jórn thought for a moment. "Not since her."

Ahead of them the tunnel branched, a shorter section running off to the right. Jórn made to duck through, then stopped. Lifting the light on his wrist he examined the wall. There was a smear of blood on the stones, a palm print and five fingers.

Nash peered around the big man. "Did the crystals get down here, do you think?"

Jórn looked at the floor. "No. Only dust."

"Then why—"

Someone screamed.

Jórn and Nash looked at one another, then back towards the darkened tunnel.

"No," said Nash.

"Yes," said Jórn.

There was another scream. It was followed by the sound of running feet.

"Fuck this!"

Jórn grabbed Nash by the arm before the smaller man could turn and flee. He dragged him kicking and cursing down the right-hand tunnel until it branched again. He listened for another scream. It came a moment later and he went towards it. Two more turns and Jórn had to press himself against the wall to keep from colliding with the two woman who went stumbling in the opposite direction.

On seeing the two armored men with their tiny caged suns, the pair ground to a halt. They sank down, hands held before their eyes. Jórn could see dirt on their faces and blood on their clothes. When neither man made a move towards them, the women shoved past and disappeared down the tunnel.

Nash sniffed, pawed at his perpetually drippy nose. "Those two've come undone. You see their eyes?"

Jórn glanced down at the smaller man. "I saw."

"There's no point trying to talk to these people. We could browbeat them all day and still not find this crystal man she's looking for. Whatever's happened to them down here has turned them into…well, you saw."

"What, you think something's hiding in these tunnels, picking off the survivors?"

"I never said that."

"You thought it though."

"How many times I got to tell you to go fuck yourself today?"

The sound of running feet came again. Jórn pointed his light down the tunnel. From the darkness burst an outstretched hand followed by the dirty face of a young man. The hand was cut and bleeding, the skin hanging in tatters. Jórn scuffed to a halt. The hand and face stopped, hovered for a moment. Jórn reached out, his own hand open, palm up. The young man's eyes went wide as he was yanked backwards, disappearing into the shadows. Screams filled the tunnel, a cacophony that buzzed in Jórn's ears and made his eyes water.

"Oh gods! Oh fuck!" Nash, the lights on his wrist pointed up at the roof of the tunnel, backed himself against the far wall. "What is that? What the hell is that?"

Jórn lifted his own arm, angled his light up.

It clung to the roof of the tunnel, the rough outline of a man encased in gilled and jagged carapace. In the jouncing, wavering light, Jórn could make out an arm, two legs, a crooked and elongated torso. The thing's head was complete to just below the eyes, then split into an insectile travesty of a mouth. The eyes themselves were black pits that sent the lights on his wrist back at Jórn in tiny shards. Held against the torso was the man that had reached for him, now more meat than man.

From where the left arm of the thing should have been there sprouted a garden of tendrils. These had been thrust into the corpse, working their way beneath its skin, burrowing through flesh and bone. They moved of their own accord, wriggling like a nest of vipers.

Nash made gobbling noises as he retreated, scraping his armored back against the tunnel wall. Jórn caught him by the arm, held him in place. The thing on the tunnel roof paused, then resumed its ministrations.

Tendrils probed and tendrils cut. The dead man lurched and shuddered. With a wet cracking noise, the corpse's chest split, ribs springing to either side. Blood stippled the floor, the walls, the front of Jórn's armor. He lifted his free hand and wiped a single droplet from the tip of his nose.

The thing on the roof lifted the corpse, pressed it to its chest. Jórn watched as the carapace grew, extending itself to cover the gaping hole it had made in the dead man. Jórn smiled as the sound of sucking and chewing replaced Nash's whimpering.

"Oh, she's going to love this," said Jórn, taking a step forward. "The Witch is absolutely going to love this."

END